Playin

Helen Dixon was born[...] read English and Philosophy at London University and is married to a geologist. They have lived abroad but now live in London with their three children and several cats.

Playing Foxes

HELEN DIXON

Flamingo
Published by Fontana Paperbacks

First published by William Collins Sons & Co. Ltd 1988

This Flamingo edition first published in 1989
by Fontana Paperbacks,
8 Grafton Street, London W1X 3LA

Flamingo is an imprint of Fontana Paperbacks,
part of the Collins Publishing Group

Typeset in Linotron Pilgrim
Printed and bound in Great Britain by
William Collins Sons & Co. Ltd, Glasgow

For my family and friends

THERE IS SOMETHING SINISTER ABOUT SNOW LIGHT . . . head-spinning as if today with the land – which is bluish-white, and the dark, overcast sky – things were turned upside down. But Anna didn't really take this in; she was too preoccupied, panicking even, and did not once stop, as she so often did these days, to look out of the window. The great cold had come in the night.

The light was wrong, and rushing she slipped again up the fifth stair, hitting her knee hard; it hurt, and she had to remind herself that she was doing this for the money. Quite simply. She switched on the lamps, checked quickly, rushed back upstairs. And still did not see the snow.

It was not yet four when the bell rang, and at the front door she caught her breath at the transformed scene, for everything was thickly white, except for the yew tree sagging onto the path.

The lamp from the road shone over the fresh snow and against the backs of the two figures standing below her so that she couldn't see their faces. In black clothes, hands by their sides, they were strangely still, yet tense as if waiting to spring up the steps. Flat snowflakes had already settled on their heads and shoulders. They bowed together. The snow fell gently round them.

The older man had a homburg hat which appeared too big for his head, and his head appeared too big for his body. He wore round glasses which added to his solemnity. 'We have come to see the room,' he said.

1

It was a relief. For a moment Anna had feared it was another visit from the Mormons who were evangelizing the area in pairs. Before she closed the door she looked out again: an excuse to regain her breath before getting on with the business. The garden was now part of a great white world which stretched down the road and beyond the houses; the falling snow already blotting out the footprints to her door.

Coming in with the tea she saw the men were still standing though the elder had removed his hat; with formality he handed her the coats, placing his briefcase by the blue chair, but sitting into its feather cushions his rather short legs shooting in front of him, he became immediately lost. Anna turned to the tray, stifling a terrible urge to laugh. Would the young man not sit too? With care, on the edge of the other chair he was, she felt, without showing any clear outward signs, dreadfully ill at ease, at a loss where to put his cup, and staring at the floor, where Anna now saw, without surprise, a wet patch from snow melted into the carpet.

What had gone wrong? She was sure she'd asked for French or Italian, as it would be nice to learn the language, but these two were surely from the Far East somewhere? The young man's spoon fell on the carpet; he didn't pick it up. The silence was unnerving. She did not see much future in him as a lodger. She sat, smiled at him, and endeavoured to be tranquil. Finally he took a noisy slurp from his tea.

Struggling out of the chair the elder man passed a visiting card and explained they were at a hotel until they could find the right place for the young man in his charge, who had learnt some English but had to learn a lot more. He looked round with deliberation. 'These are your husband's books? That is good. And . . . ' he added, turning over papers before him, ' . . . he is Dean, Mr Dean.' Anna was intrigued to think that Gregory's name was down there in foreign script and was about to correct the 'is' for 'was' when she was asked did she go to church and did she have a tub?

Anna had indeed gone to church since Gregory had died,

partly to see if there might be an answer there, but also for something to do on those awful Sundays with the children. One didn't admit to that. 'And I don't think I have a tub,' she said, puzzled. She looked sideways at the young man. One thing: if he stayed he wasn't going to be noisy.

There was a long pause. Physically, she realized, they bothered her. The older man's skin was the colour of old piano keys. His hair stuck out like a brush. His teeth were large and he made a sucking noise with them while he consulted his notebook. 'How then do you clean your body?'

'I have a shower,' she said stiffly, 'and a bath.'

'Ah, you have a bath.' There followed some explanation which the young man heard in silence.

'You would permit use of your bath?'

'Of course.'

What a peculiar language! A staccato rattling sound. Anna cleared her throat, gave a little sigh. No matter what she did, a tight smile kept creeping on her face. No one was smiling back. Playing with the visiting card she found it written in English on the other side. This, then, was Mr Otaki, from Japan. It was both irritating and unnerving to sit so quiet in her own house. She felt ignored. (You'll regret it, her mother had decided. It's my bed, she'd said back, so I'll lie on it. Anyway, I have to do something. And taking lodgers is the simplest solution.) It was going on for longer than anyone would have thought to explain about the bath, and information of what they would eat. To all of this the young man assented with scarcely audible little noises, still staring at his feet. What had she let herself in for? She was glad when she could take them upstairs to the room, where with the same thoroughness he'd already shown Mr Otaki produced a camera, and a flash, told Anna to stand at the foot of the bed . . . where she smiled once more. Several pictures of the room, and herself in it were taken.

It was completely dark by now. Outside the snow was thicker, and large flakes were sticking to the cold window-panes. 'It is beautifu,' the young man agreed shyly.

3

Did he have much snow in his part of Japan? But this was all she got out of him. If permission was given, the other man said, then they would return next week.

What permission?

We have to ask Tokyo.

Be damned to Tokyo, she was thinking, watching them walk with precise and careful steps to the road. Although she was chilled, she lingered behind the shelter of the front door. There was a north-east wind blowing directly into the house; it was scooping the top off the lying snow and relaying it up the steps in a smooth mat. The garden looked so different in a way which was disturbing – the familiar shapes changed, almost displaced and rearranged – as if it had already been taken over and transformed by the Japanese.

'I don't like them,' Janet said, the new neighbour. As usual she'd come round, and Anna, always grateful, was even more so today for her cheerful presence, sitting there, her neat little face rising out of an immense cowl-necked sweater.

Anna had never met any before.

'Neither have I, but from what one's heard . . . '

But the War was a long time ago and they seemed to have gone in for shopkeeping ever since, which must make them as safe and dull as the dear English, so Anna thought.

'Oh well, if you've made up your mind.'

'I haven't, but I've never had lodgers before, so how can one tell?'

'It's better to have someone from a bit closer, say France. And you are having a man, aren't you? A girl will be forever washing her hair and having her periods. A man's definitely better, and if he was nice just think what might happen . . . '

4

'What might happen?'

Some of Janet's jauntiness had gone, but she took a little breath and hurrying on, 'Anna, you're too young . . . I mean you have to start living again for yourself. And we were saying anyway . . . ' she went on, her voice rather weak, bending over to smooth out her legwarmers,' . . . you need to meet some men . . . '

Anna stood to make coffee as she discovered she was shaking again; occasionally her body still let her down.

'They're very clean, aren't they?' Janet was asking behind her back. 'Mind you,' she said as if she had given the matter some thought, 'that will cost you more money in heating water. And they're small. I saw a film once and they're all small. Very short legs.'

'Oh good. That'll save six inches off each sheet I have to wash.'

Janet started giggling; she did so want things to get better. Both Dave and she . . .

Anna yet again struggled with the temptation to describe to this kind friend how one day, finding her weeping (just self-pity, only that), Dave had tried to comfort her, and that no-man's-land that one had assumed lay between compassionate and sexual feelings appeared not to exist. Her own hunger then had distressed her, and worried her since.

Stretching, warming her fingers round her cup, Dave's wife was looking at Anna with those unclouded eyes of hers. She made Anna feel ten years older. 'I do so admire you. I'd hate to have strange people using my . . . house. But you – ' she started off again, 'Oh Hell, sorry . . . ' and Anna went off to answer the phone.

And when she returned to see Janet already struggling into her fur coat: 'The college says, there's no Hungarians, no Poles. Lots of Arabs.'

Her fur matched Janet's hair. 'Arabs have lots of money. But chauvinist. They see women as camels, don't they?'

*

5

The snow continued to fall. It was going to be a hard winter. She sent the children out to find wood in the local park and while they were out stuffed more newspaper round the sash windows. The Bursar from the college rang saying she'd wanted to see Anna to put her in the picture about the young Japanese. She sounded worried. What with trying to keep Arabs and Asians warm, perhaps it would be all right . . . ? 'Professor' Otaki rang; he had taken bad cold. He also sounded anxious, with intentions to revisit and talk with Mr Dean as it was important to meet him, but he was unwell, his charge not yet able to move about alone . . . but in any case Mr Dean was not there?

No, Mr Dean was not there.

Then could he take it that Hideo could come in two days? They might meet again if his health allowed it. Could she tell him what they did at weekends? Did they make trips? He sneezed loudly, blew his nose over the telephone. It was most important to study. Tokyo insisted on learning English.

Anna said they would do all they could to help him.

There was such a long pause that she asked in the end: 'Professor, are you all right?'

'Ahhh . . . it is great pity I cannot talk with Mr Dean. You must explain to him that America is bad place for young man. He is not used to rough places. Too many bad people. Also they . . . ' there was another long pause, 'they do not have such a correct life. Please make sure he follows correct behaviour.'

'I don't know what you mean by that.'

'Ahhh . . . correct like an Englishman. Polite and clean. He knows what to do. He must follow good principles. And be

6

quiet. This is important. Do you understand?' The voice on the other end of the phone sounded exhausted as if each expression had had to be carved out of something solid and carted about and rearranged. Professor Otaki repeated that he regretted not being able to leave the hotel, his health, the bad weather . . . then he added: 'Tokyo approves the room. They have seen the photographs,' and rang off.

How could that have happened in so short a time?

Most of what Professor Otaki assumed were Gregory's books were in fact Anna's; and mostly second-hand. She liked reading: it was something you could do by yourself, not have to share like television, often spoiled in the past by comments from Gregory, and now by interruptions from the children. Gregory had built shelves over one wall, and here the oddballs and misfits sat colourfully enough among his engineering books. Somewhere there should be something about the Japanese.

But the single-tone pictures from an ancient encyclopedia were not helpful . . . the Japanese have 'small black eyes, long black hair, sallow or dirty olive complexion. They are a feeble folk with contracted chest, and marked tendency to anaemia (due to the poor diet, with a little fish or pickled vegetables) and they have three curses in their life: earth-quakes, fire and Father.' This unflattering description was reinforced by some old sepia photographs of different classes of people in various postures but all determinedly mournful. She could not take them seriously.

While she was musing about this the telephone rang; a hesitation was followed by a silvery voice, a voice of quite unlikely sweetness, asking her to do them the honour of confirming that she was Mrs Dean, and that this was her house, and that her number. The formality had Anna almost bowing over the receiver. She did as asked, and waited. But after a while decided that they had been cut off, yet the phone had a sort of occupied feel as if someone was listening intently at the other end. Anna repeated her number clearly

7

with that weary patience that mothers with children quickly acquire; again she had the impression that someone was holding their breath miles away when the sweet voice broke in to say: 'This is Tokyo. Thank you for being so good to answer, Mrs Dean.' And the line went dead.

That day the sun shone for the first time in a week out of a sky of palest grey, and threw a light into the house bright enough to hurt the eyes. The snow looked set hard like icing yet was soft enough for small birds to leave delicate tracks over its surface. Still there was no word. Could the young Japanese have taken fright and flown straight back? Anna grew afraid for her sanity at times like these when a reverse of one sort or another could throw her into a rage, internally. That it was something to do with having to manage on her own was likely and she wondered whether Gregory had felt helpless like this when faced with bills. He had never given any sign other than a tightening of the lips. But then, it had taken so long for her to find out how much he hid.

When the Bursar rang it was to say that Professor Otaki had left the country and the young man was on his way in the next hour and um, how could they say this, the young man it had been stressed had been reared delicately, he was a bit 'sensitive', he had to be kept quiet. Anna's heart sank; was she supposed to mother this creature? It was possible he didn't want it, maybe he was dying to get away from home. 'I'm afraid Professor Otaki seemed to think my husband was still alive. I'm sorry, but I didn't put him wise.' She couldn't think why not.

'It's funny you should say that. You see we had a great deal of difficulty. I mean it's the wrong time of year and our quotas

8

are full, but when we were asked to make a special case . . .
anyway, to be honest, you were our last hope. But if you're
changing your mind . . .'

There was such a strong feeling of embarrassment coming
off the line that Anna (who had been wavering) reassured
her at once, no she would not let them down, but had the
Bursar put the parents in the picture about her; she didn't
want there to be any misunderstandings.

There was a longish pause. 'I didn't exactly spell it out. I
mean, I just had to find somewhere. It would not have
helped us to refuse a place. You know what I mean?'

'No, actually.'

A deep sigh. 'We have a lot of privately placed, rich young
people; they come for a European education to acquire a bit
of polish, that sort of thing. They come from a protected
environment, and their families are understandably very
anxious about their welfare, and coming from some count-
ries, of course . . . the comparison, England is very safe, but – '
she cleared her throat, 'it's an anxiety for us. Young people
are young people and there are times – '

'But you didn't actually tell them that I was a widow?'

'It slipped my mind.' The voice tailed off, then rallied in
irritation. 'I mean they are so difficult to talk to, those
Japanese. So oblique.' Spitting out the word as if she had at
last landed on the right expression. 'Tell me now if you
think you can't cope. Because there will be trouble over this
if I have to start again with this man.' Her voice had
hardened. 'I have to tell you though that if you do feel that
you cannot take this student then I won't be able to find you
anyone else.'

Alarmed, Anna said she expected it would work out.

'And let's keep this between ourselves about your situation. After all, it's the other side of the world, isn't it? Why
should it make any difference? You won't ring tomorrow and
say no? How can it matter there isn't another man in the
house? You can give him more time.'

But there was a ring at the door. 'I haven't any choice,' Anna said. 'I think he's already arrived.'

Something about his fare had so impressed the taxi-man that he not only staggered up the front path through the snow with several cases, but also crashed up the stairs with them as well, leaving snow on the carpet as he went. At the door a twenty-pound note exchanged hands and only the slippery state of the steps prevented a quick getaway.

'That's too much,' Anna said firmly.

The taxi-man continued belligerent. Listen, it was bloody slippy out there . . . All this time the young man stood silently by, no expression at all on his face.

'You can't rip him off like that,' she said again fiercely, surprised at herself. 'Where did you pick him up?'

'Hilton. So he can afford it. Friend of yours, is he?'

'He's going to live here, not that it's any of your business, and we want change, please.'

The driver said we all have our own way of earning a living, and dropped a five-pound note on the floor between them.

'Sorry about that,' she was saying as she shut the door. She was flushed. The Japanese gave a little bow. Wouldn't he like some tea, and would he like to unpack, and be quiet in his room? Again he gave a bow; he said yes, he said thank you, and went upstairs. Silence filled the house.

Three hours later the money was still there and both Nicholas and Fay, home from school, had noticed it. He must be awful, Nicholas decided, and he didn't like Japanese.

'You don't know anything about them,' Fay said.

'I do. They used to torture people by burying them alive up to their necks in sand. There's a film about it.'

'Nick,' Anna interrupted sharply, 'you are not to talk about that. It's got nothing to do with anything. And this is my way of getting some more money, otherwise,' she said lowering her voice, and getting suddenly weepy again, 'we are going to be in a hell of a mess.' Wiping her nose she saw their eyes on her, anxious, waiting to see which way things would go. 'He's been up there since he arrived. Go and say hello. Be polite. They are very polite. Say: "Would you like some tea?" Clearly. Right?'

Nick said he'd gone in, and there the Japanese was sitting cross-legged on the bed, and he'd said (when asked) yes. But after ten minutes had gone by Anna put the tea on a tray. It was Fay's turn. 'But he's not ill,' she grumbled, 'why the fuss?' Because they had to look after him, that's why. Some minutes later Fay came down the stairs clumping on each step. 'He just said thank you, and I'm not doing that again. I felt so stupid.' So Nick said she was stupid, and they had a scrap. Anna wanted to hit them.

The hours drifted towards supper time, but there was no sign, no sound. Foreign students are expected to eat what their hosts eat but she did wonder if a few concessions would be a good idea after Nick, as was his habit, had peered into the pots with: 'You're not giving him that!'

'It's a stew. It's hot, and nourishing. And cheap.'

'It's all in bits.'

'Go, Nick, there's a love.'

He whinged. She could go, or Fay could go. Why? Because she'd asked him. She was apprehensive, and trying to hide it. As one moved between the stove and sink one could feel the drop in temperature. The cold penetrated the glass, reaching into the room, her fingers shrinking at the touch of the taps; the light from the kitchen went only a little way into the frozen dark outside.

Supper ready they sat at the table and waited. After some time Anna with a heightened colour decided to eat. The smell of food was circling round the house and couldn't be ignored. Perhaps he found it all so appalling he didn't dare come down. This at any rate was Nick's theory. 'Perhaps he doesn't like it here. And can I have my room back?'

It was sometime into the evening when the door opened where the three of them were watching television and the young man stood at the doorway. 'I want bath,' he said.

11

Ah . . . of course, rather funny, but in most English houses the bathroom is upstairs but their house was rather old, and hadn't a modern one and therefore the bathroom was right there off the hall, and did he want towels?

Nick seeing an advantage slipped past her at this point and handed the money over. The young man made a curious gesture with his hand, a sort of pushing away. He shut himself in. They listened. There was silence, then some tentative splashes.

'If I'd have had it I'd have shared,' Fay insisted hopefully. So they sat resentfully with Anna, Nick with the money firmly in his grasp, until after more time than one would have thought at all necessary had passed, and then the door opened once more.

Anna had started up at this apparition. A cloud of steam hung behind him; his hair stuck spikily round his skull, but worse, he was dressed in a kind of stretch towelling of palest blue zipped from crutch to neck, with socks. He bowed, tried to speak. An explosion behind her Anna knew was her son beating the cushions with his fists while he choked with laughter. She tried to warn Nick but this terrible smile took over her face; she felt Fay slip her arms round her waist and peep out from the safety of her mother's back, from where she smiled winningly, 'Hallo.'

The Japanese bowed again. 'Haro. Bery preased to meet you.' Then he bowed to Anna and handed her the towels, neatly folded and very wet. He tried again but the words would not come. Anna could feel Fay at her side shaking with silent laughter. The wet towels were beginning to drip unpleasantly on her feet. Eventually he raised his head. 'I thank you for my Ingrish bath. Hope you have good sreep,' and padded up the stairs. Both the children went off into fresh shrieks as Anna hastily shut the door. He must feel insulted. 'There, now you've given yourself hiccoughs.' To herself she said that he had been accepted.

*

12

Anna had never thought of herself as anything but a hopeful
person. She had wanted to be happy. And indeed had been
happy enough until the start of the bad days when Gregory
was beginning to be ill, but she had thought he was going
mad. Those days had trimmed them in bit by bit, contracted
their world which had stayed shrunk to this point where she
was imprisoned inside her home, and herself. Her daily task
caring for her children. A small domestic life she had now.

She made the decision to leave well alone in the morning –
always a bad time – but also she felt bad about the previous
evening. One could never tell how people would react.
Would he eat breakfast? They looked doubtfully at the
marmalade. The phone rang – strange time – and Fay
answering it on her way out to school held the receiver
towards her mother, making faces. 'Really Fay, you're ten
now, ask who it is.' Violently she shook her head. 'Tokyo.'

'Ah . . . ' came the silvery voice, 'this is Tokyo, may I
speak with Mrs Dean, please? Is Mr Ishida living at this place?'
Puzzled, Anna replied, and was asked to hold on. She waited.
She waited for what seemed a long time and began to wonder
how much this was costing. 'Mrs Dean. This is Tokyo again.
Thank you.' That was it. Anna stood holding the telephone
until the buzzer on it sounded.

Janet came round mid-morning. Anna was grateful to
Janet who had taken up with her after Gregory died when
other friends, curiously, and in a way Anna could not
understand, had retreated.

'Someone rang from Tokyo this morning.'

'How odd. What did they say?'

'They didn't say anything.'

13

'How very odd.' Janet appeared restless, moving to the kitchen door, looking out, and not really attending to Anna's descriptions. But she said she thought Anna had a problem on her hands. No sign of him yet? She stayed longer than usual, but in the end was getting up to go when he came in. He bowed and immediately left the room.

'There now,' in exasperation, 'you've frightened him off, Janet.'

'Good God, no one can be that shy. I hope you haven't a nutcase on your hands and a Japanese nutcase at that. What's his name anyway?'

And that was another stupid thing; that she'd forgotten.

Anna busied herself round the house. There was no sound. Was he still in the house? Her memories of a spirit slowly leaving were making her shudder, but it was also the cold. She hated cold. Yet here was another human being upstairs, lost perhaps, lonely. Ill at ease she tiptoed round. The day wore on and there was still no sign, until Nick returned from school and suggested they go up and ask Hideo to come down for tea.

There was the tray from yesterday, untouched. Curiously, no unpacking seemed to have taken place. Could he dislike it here so much? The bed looked as if someone had had a fight with it; what looked like the previous day's wear lay on the floor, but at the side of the washbasin was laid out a toothbrush, toothpicks, a new tube of toothpaste parallel and a flannel neatly folded in four. Behind this was a box of pressed cardboard full of small squares of fine white paper. It had to be at the very moment she picked this up that he came in.

'I came for the tray. Would you like some fresh tea?'

Again they waited. He did say yes, Anna insisted. Perhaps she spoke too fast; if they shouted *tea*! you know, like you do to us . . .

'You'll do no such thing, Fay.'

It was dinner time before he appeared. Rubbing his hands and making noises about cold, he was asked hadn't he wanted any tea to which he replied yes, as usual, and Anna saw that

14

politeness was not getting them anywhere. Do you want rice, therefore was as basic as anyone could get, and it worked for he straightaway helped himself and began immediately to eat, bent over his plate and making loud noises as he did so. Anna brought from her armoury a look which froze anything less than two paces away. The children recognized it as such and sat still until she had served herself, which coincided with the time when their lodger came to a halt. When he rose and left.

Again the telephone rang that following breakfast. The same gentle woman's voice repeated: this is Tokyo. Wait a moment, please. It occurred to Anna that messages were being relayed after translation. Could she say what he ate last evening meal? He ate rice. Another long pause, then: 'Rice is good. Thank you.'

It was not surprising that she still felt edgy, for he padded around the house in his socks giving her small shocks. They would smile, he would retreat, murmuring something. There was some perverse law at work that dictated they would come out of a room at the same time, meet on the stairs, arrive at the lavatory simultaneously, and she would really have to say something (how embarrassing) about shutting the door there: he seemed to have no feelings of modesty whatever.

How cold! It penetrated through to the bones. The intense cold as so often in England had excited people: it changed the predictable pattern. They walked in the middle of the roads on a par, for once, with the cars. Discomfort united them. One or two of the men had reminded Anna to do things to the pipes, and neighbours either side, who she scarcely knew, had

15

helped her when she started to chip the pavement ice. One welcomed the friendliness, for it was strange enough having some other person perpetually in her home. It was Janet who pointed out this was the first time she'd had another adult male living in the house since Gregory's death. Since those first months of stunned shock followed by the time of guilt and mourning, Anna had found that bereavement had many unexpected and desolating aspects: that a form of relief (which looked like a feeling of being free) appeared to exist somewhere; that friends acted in ways that didn't add up. She now began to wonder why Janet came round so much. She came to talk, and stayed too long. She sat there now smoking, her fingers fidgeting with her hair.

'They rang *again*! How weird! And he asked for soup? For breakfast!'

'He ate toast. Without butter. And he hates sweet things like honey. I hope I survive this.'

'There must be lots of money there if they can ring to find what he's had for dinner.'

'I hope I never get that possessive. And I haven't a clue what he thinks. His face is a blank. There's just one thing we've found out *not* to do: if you ask him things politely you'll not get the right answer because he'll always say yes.'

'That's not logical. It's all upside down, for heaven's sake. Does he seem stupid?'

Anna shrugged. She didn't know.

'Oh Anna, I hope they didn't send him away because he's dim; you know, thick,' her voice rising, 'well, subnormal!'

How could one tell? If one could not talk or explain oneself then all was mystery, and his eyes – one couldn't guess anything from them.

'Anna . . . ' Janet's voice had a different tone, as if she had something on her mind, and she rubbed a space on the misted pane and peeped through, and shivered. Yet when she moved back she was smiling again. 'Did you see the fox? The cold, I

16

suppose. It's been seen in the back gardens several times. You'd better not let your kitten out.'

'Go on. A fox is not interested in things like that.'

'Want a bet? They're sneaky.'

When she saw the state of the room Anna again had a surge of anger which left her hot and breathless. It took some minutes to calm herself down. By the washbasin were laid out the same things as before. Everything was scattered everywhere; small empty sachets with Japanese lettering screwed up all over the floor; no clue as to what they may have contained. Nothing to show what kind of person she had taken into her house. She needed a job; something to take her out of the house. But she wasn't ready; she clung to the walls; it was still, in so many different ways, still too cold out there.

It gave her such a start when she turned to find him at the door of the room. How he crept about!

'You have come home early.'

He gave a little bow. '*Hai*, yes, I have no crass.'

She gestured round the room. She noticed how his hands would hang at his side as he inclined his head, a north and south movement, but no east and west.

'Can I call you Hideo? Please call me Anna.'

'Prease.'

Taking a breath: 'I am going to have some tea. You like tea, don't you?' Then seeing his baffled face: 'Do you like tea?'

'I rike tea.'

Together in the kitchen she stopped herself just in time from adding milk. For the first time she saw a smile, and encouraged, asked him if he understood better?

He produced a book, the English on one page; its

translation into characters on the other. Carefully he read out a question, but didn't follow its answer; and when she pointed at the equivalent she realized exactly how incomprehensible it was. She herself could not begin to fathom the signs.

'You give me ressions.'

She was not going to get caught doing the college's job. 'Perhaps, but I'm very busy.'

'I see.' And he got up immediately to go so that she felt she'd snubbed him and she said, 'Oh, there was a call. From Tokyo.' He stood still in that strange way he had. 'This morning,' she added. He still stood irresolute as if the questions he wanted to ask were just too complicated. And then gave up.

Hideo kept a strict timetable. Anna received her first payment and crunched triumphantly through the snow to show it. Dave unfortunately was there. No, there was nothing bothering her, but she found herself talking too much and telling the silly story of braising some leeks which Hideo had sucked up whole. 'Quite extraordinary. He didn't bite them once. And all right for you to laugh, but you know Nick, you know what eight-year-olds are like, he did the same just to dare me to tell him off.'

'And did you?'

Anna winced. Afterwards she had.

'Perhaps they eat noisily to show appreciation, like the Arabs belch.'

'He does that as well.'

'Until his English improves – '

'Oh we're making progress. He always says yes to everything but . . . '

18

There was a glint in Dave's eye. 'That's nice. What's he like as a bloke, Anna?'

'He's really just a boy. First time away from home. He sits in front of the television with the kids and laughs when they laugh. We're very merry.'

Dave said warmly that he was glad things were working well. 'And it gives you something different to talk about – ' Then he realized.

Oh, Anna said, ah, as the tears came. Janet said sharply: 'David, you fool!' But Anna had got up and left. Too swiftly, for she slipped farcically outside the door on the ice; she sat there going, ah, ah, her skirt round her hips. David helped her up. 'Anna, love, I'm sorry, I'm really sorry.' He held her. 'No bones broken?' his arm firmly round her, pulling her to him. Anna gave a little shake. 'I'll see you over the road.'

'There's no need.'

'I insist. I'll see her to the house,' he called back to his wife.

He saw her back, and into the house and once there: 'Anna, I'm sorry. Say you forgive me,' holding her, and looking at her with maudlin eyes.

'It was just a passing moment. You don't have to kiss me better.'

She was in fact lying in bed going over things in her mind when the telephone rang on Sunday morning and there was the familiar voice asking charmingly for Mr Ishida. It took some time for Hideo to emerge, and for a while all she heard was him saying 'Hai' over and over again. Then suddenly he roused and a torrent of sound came up the stairs and round her door. All Japanese sounded bad-tempered.

19

All morning he sat looking out at the garden, but she asked no questions. Fay thought he was sad. How could she tell? In the end he went with them into the park where he joined the children in making little hard snowballs out of the diminishing piles at the side of the paths. Watching them, Anna felt maternal towards them all. It was beginning to work; he giggled as they threw ball after ball to smash against a tree, really there was a lot of the child in him still. But things changed abruptly: intent now, he took careful aim at the ducks standing on the ice of the pond. The birds tried to take off, slithered, braked, slipped and slid into the hole opened for them in the ice, quacking angrily. The children indignantly stopped him from throwing more. He looked excited. But they ignored him, running ahead in the dusk. Anna, also annoyed, tried to encourage him to walk with her. Large flakes of snow were beginning to twist down from the sky. Hideo looked at his shoes; she set off after the children and he followed at some distance, planting his feet one after the other as if on a forced march.

Sunday afternoon was the time when weekly Anna's parents checked up on her. As the youngest of their children they never really expected her to cope; the latest to marry, the first to be left on her own. Though they had not been much drawn to this son-in-law they still felt it shocking he had been struck down in his prime. Now out of affection, out of duty they would make the fifty-mile run to see them all. This afternoon the alibi of bad road conditions was accepted; and a telephone call did instead.

'Your father asks whether you haven't taken on more than you can chew.' A deep sigh. 'Is it all right? I mean, saying "perfectly" doesn't tell us anything much. Oh well. I suppose you know your own business best, Anna. Are you eating properly? That's one good thing, you do have to make a meal.'

Anna asked after her mother's back, her father's cough; she asked after everyone. There was nothing new. She decided to wait until Hideo was, so to speak, more anglicized before allowing them to meet. But they're not intolerant, she was thinking, looking out over the dusk-shadowed garden, only they get so embarrassed. A russet shape moved towards the back hedge where the abutting fence was beginning to come down. 'Come quick! Look Hideo, a fox! The first time I've ever seen one. Can you see it?' But he didn't move. 'It's all right,' she said, 'you can look,' for the fox had stayed still, its muzzle slightly raised, the ears pricked forward and the tail down but clearly in view against what was left of the snow. 'They don't usually come into the town.' There was a certain pride in being able to display such an unusual event. 'It must be this dreadful cold,' she went on but to the children, for Hideo had shaken his head and gone to his room. It was curiously disappointing. Yet he had liked their kitten.

And that following morning Anna merely knocked on the door, 'Telephone!' and left it lying. He talked, he even laughed.

'So everything's all right?' the Bursar stated rather than asked. Her office spoke money, not only in the carpets and such, but also in that attentiveness that meant someone cleaned there often. In keeping with this she was smartly, even aggressively dressed.

'We get rather a lot of telephone calls.'

'Oh?'

'Every day so far. Every morning at half-seven exactly. From Japan.'

'Oh dear. That's not at all usual.' She bent over papers, Yes, they now realized his English was less than would normally qualify, but . . . It was a special case. Anna found this

21

irritating, but did not say so; resolve was forming in her mind which was no one's business but her own.

'Can you tell me something about him? His parents?'

The Bursar frowned and turned away. 'There's really nothing to tell. Ask him.'

'But his English is . . . He's so shy' (for it would not do to complain). 'I mean who are they? Surely you must ask yourself – '

'I don't know anything.' She gave a small dismissing smile: it was none of Anna's business. Whence the mystery? Anna shrugged. She supposed they had a right not to divulge, but it was curious. It did not promise well.

The Bursar had been fiddling with papers. 'Money? You got the money? Good. There might be a little extra to come. If you could help with conversation? We do . . .' (again looking at the papers, or appearing to) ' . . . yes, we do appear to have some extra, put aside.'

'It's hardly conversation with – '

'He understands far more than you think, I daresay.' She stood and practically propelled Anna from the room. 'See me next week if you are bothered. No, make it a month from now. The whole business is something of a trial, frankly.'

'The fox was in the garden.'

'Was it, Fay?'

'I think he's hungry. Can we put something out?'

'I'll think about it. That's enough about the fox. What did you do today, Hideo?'

'Ressions. I go to ressions,' and when she shook her head gently he rose. 'I work.' And his light stayed on long after midnight.

In this curious disjointed way more than the week seemed to have passed. Anna looking into the hall mirror to see what other people saw, found a frown, a sad droop had taken hold. This was not how she wanted to be seen. This was not how she wanted to be. Then felt herself watched. Hideo standing on the stairs; one could not tell a thing from that impassive face but he had been there perhaps some time. At this moment she felt the space there was between him and his home, the oddness of her bannisters, the unfamiliarity of the furniture, the foreignness of that dark Edwardian hall with its exotic stained glass, even the light of England outside which today was grey with a thaw and rain falling. 'Oh, excuse me, prease.'

'It is raining I'm afraid.' How shy he made her.

'Oh, I have umbrerra!'

She didn't laugh; as if some hand had gently pressed the back of her head she found herself give a little nod, '*Sayonara.*' And he grinned with pleasure, his face changed, and went off lightly into the sleety rain.

This then was the state of Tokyo in 1982: that in their homes the Japanese have very little space; that flush lavatories are in only 25 per cent of homes and the 'honeycart' still goes round to collect the nightly sewage; that many roads of the main streets are not even metalled; that there are whole sets of flats without lifts. This in the country which has the highest GNP in the world.

'Is this all?' Such a curious collection at the library: books with no connection with each other by business men for others with statistics and graphs; or refined descriptions of the tea ceremony, or the practices of Zen. And in another part

23

of the library, books of paintings, of gardens, of flowers, and the arrangement of flowers; and somewhere again dark books written by survivors from the last war. Just one or two of each of these rapidly produced a peculiar sensation in Anna's head, a kind of mental nausea. She bent over the books hopelessly wondering if the ordinary person did exist; she'd never before realized there were so many Japanese, or that they were so indistinguishable one from the other. And what one didn't expect, this odd presentation: noblemen appeared now to be the heads of industry; their writers distinguished by the manner of their deaths (mostly suicide); their women all were smiling, and those that were not turned out to be female impersonators. It was all most bewildering, not least her own reactions. She had looked at the pictures of gardens, immediately impressed, then sitting back asked why she was bothered still, and realized that this pinching and pruning and cutting back of nature cut too deeply into something she subscribed to. But did not know what.

'People aren't that different, basically. It would be more exciting if they were,' so Janet said. 'God, most people are so boring. Don't you find?'

Anna had come slowly back; she had talked, as was clear, more than Janet would any longer tolerate. 'I really can't work up much enthusiasm, Japan's an awful long way away. I mean they're obviously clever, but Dave says they got a leg up from the Americans. And they're so rich now. We dropped a bomb on them; and now we're paying for it. For Heaven's sake, he's only your lodger. Keep your mind straight. He's there for you to earn some money.'

True, Hideo was not a civilization; but he was strange, unexplained. She no longer felt the same woman since Gregory's death, this was to be expected, but now the house itself felt different, even the road unfamiliar, distorted somehow. It was disturbing. And seeing the children coming down the road her mind took a jump to the game of blind-man's-bluff, to that moment when, the blind off, you find

24

yourself facing a different direction than the one you thought, and you feel for some moments the world tilting and taking you with it. The sun rises in the east, and eastwards from Japan was her west. Poor young man; she must make an effort for him.

Back home her mood changed abruptly. Hideo had taken his bath. A pool of water lay under and beyond the bathroom door, spreading into the hall. Inside awash and dripping, except at the window where it was freezing. Her knowledge of the bathing habits as recent as that morning's reading, Anna did not feel justified in complaining, but as she bent mopping and wringing, the pose of subservience riled her. More so when she found he had been trimming his hair. The cut hairs had a life of their own; tough, straight, black and springy, they worked their way through the cloth, stuck stubbornly in the spaces between the tiles. Seized with loathing – it reminded her too clearly of those last few months of cleaning after Gregory – so the Japanese think it dirty to sit in one's own filthy bath water! Right. What about this? And that horror of impurity, illness and blood – basic to the Shinto religion – how does that tie in with pernickety habits with food, his way of eating with his mouth open, his forgetting to shut the lavatory door, his way . . . ?

They have a reputation along with the Chinese for being inscrutable. So far he was living up to it. And Japanese women have a reputation for being sweet and compliant. Hideo had a mother perhaps who was like this and cleaned up after him. But he was in London now.

In clear printing, and not taking too much thought, for she knew she'd then tear them up, Anna wrote several notices: Please close the door when using the lavatory (WC). Please point the shower-head towards the wall. Please wipe/hang things up after you. 'After you'? she paused over, then shrugged. He could carry his phrase book round and translate as he went.

'And what do you think *you're* doing?' to her son that evening. She pointed to: 'Gentlemen please lift seat.' The door had also been left open.

He denied he was a gentleman.

'Then work on it.'

'You're like school. Answers for everything.' Then he burst into tears, shouting: 'Daddy wouldn't have!'

During that night there was another deceitful fall in temperature; in the morning the world outside was once more white with thick frost. Woken early from cold and peering at the garden, Anna thought she saw the fox. With the real dawn it began again to snow. She could sense that today her spirits would have great trouble in rising, and when the breakfast telephone call came her irritation kept her short with Hideo. Oh, that delicate light voice! But of what could she complain? In her bedroom as she pulled back her bedclothes the empty space unruffled by the side of hers perhaps gave her the impulse. Who could it be? A girl left behind, lovelorn if not neurotic? In any case she reached for the other telephone put in when Gregory got ill, lifting it with care, holding the mouthpiece away from her.

'*Moshi, moshi,*' Hideo said. ' . . . *Hai* . . . *hai.*' But the woman's voice on the other end was that of what? A woman distraught? Annoyed? Or just anxious? There was a babbling run to the voice, high, shrill even. But the language was so unknown one could not interpret even the tone. She could have been hysterical, yet Hideo's replies were, as usual, clipped and short and gave no hint of feeling; just the minimum of response.

'Now I go to Rondon. With others. I eat.'

Pleased for him; was the news from Japan all right? she went on to ask with that winning smile that used to get her answers to questions. He didn't reply; in fact gave no sign of having heard.

*

26

Her instincts had been right. Later that day Anna opened the door to a cheerful glowing woman, soberly dressed in what turned out to be the uniform of a tax-inspector. Anna stared down at the demand forthwith for two thousand pounds. Back tax. Owing. The insult of it all was the questions asked not too subtly to elicit whether she had been 'deserted'. Someone had slipped up. 'I didn't know he was in such a mess,' she said, depressed. Not many wives did, apparently. And had she anyone living with her now? No, just her children. With a bleak certainty that she really was on her own, and that the children had only her to sort things out.

'How on earth am I supposed to get that sort of money?'

Time would be given, of course.

Only when the woman was going down the steps did Anna remember Hideo; staring down the path (damned if she was going to call her back) she saw footsteps in the snow by the hedge. They could have been a dog's, of course, but she decided they belonged to the fox. She liked that. She liked him for his wildness here in the city. She admired his cheek.

The children especially annoying when they returned from school, Anna drifted away from their chatter to scrutinize once more a list of sums in her head. She hadn't liked the discovery that some people were snooping on her life, that there were entries, and numbers and codes belonging to her marriage time which people were still busying themselves with. For her it appeared that debts were not so easily cancelled out as lives. She came to, to hear the two squabbling.

'Anyway, he isn't yellow.'

Nick banging his spoon. 'Mummeee . . . Listen! Why is being yellow being a coward?'

'I don't know.'

'It's silly. It's stupid.'

'He isn't yellow, is he? He's cream, sort of tanned,' Fay was saying with a judicious and annoying air of being right. 'Like everyone else. He hasn't proper eyebrows, though.'

Nick said he had.

'And something's funny with his eyes.'

Nick was silent about this statement which he wanted to agree with if only his sister hadn't said it. But in Anna there was a realization that she hadn't studied Hideo. Quite why she couldn't say.

'They're very black.'

'His hair is really black.'

'His feet are small.'

'No they're not. They're the same size as Mummy's. I measured them,' said Fay, and Anna was beginning to smile at this when Nick said: not as big as Daddy's, and began to cry over his cake. Ah, she said, scooping him up in her arms, 'You're doing well you two, being my eyes and taking things in. Come and see if we can find Mr Fox this evening. He may be in the garden now it's dusk.'

Together they looked out. It had stopped snowing. A lone blackbird in the cherry tree was making his territorial song; no other birds took up the call and soon he flew off. Some wind made the bushes move and the snow slithered softly from them onto the ground; she held the children to her by the chilly window-panes. No fox.

She was liable for all that money and couldn't rid her mind of it. The house had developed permanent pockets of cold which stayed like presences at the bend of the stairs, on the landing near the bedroom door; and in the kitchen a draft caught the ankles up to her shins from the cat-door, a spear shape cut from the key-hole always when the wind was from the northeast. Thinking and going about habitual tasks, it was some time before she realized the telephone had not, this morning, rung. And going into Hideo's room she found it had been made tidy. Clothes arranged with scrupulous care, everything hung, the bed rolled back. And on the table, his work. He had of course not only to learn language but script. In large ill-formed letters, like a child's he had written a series of phrases: 'I go, I am going, I am going with people, I am going alone.' When he put down his pencil and pen he put them precisely parallel with the paper. A white rubber lay at right angles to their points. There was nothing to do but empty away the many sachets. As she tipped them into the bin white powder fell with them. Medicine, she thought, for something or other.

That night Anna woke from some nightmare and half awake was wondering how the subconscious could really work when it seemed so banal, when she was shaken wide awake by a scream. No, it wasn't a scream, but a howl. On the landing the frightened children were already coming for her. They surveyed the road. One or two lights were on. The howl must have caught an echo for it rolled back and forth between the walls of the houses and repeated itself. It sounded like someone in intense pain. The yowl rose in tone. A door opened in the road. Other lights went on. The men were seeing to it. The yowl changed into a prolonged yelp as if the animal were trying to drag itself away with terrible injuries. It died away into the distance, and there was silence. Outside, men in various bits of clothing, some with torches, were making gestures of helplessness and desire to get out of the cold. Anna, downstairs to get warm drinks, found she had a quite inexplicable desire to laugh. She lingered before going back to bed, content with the knowledge that no more was being demanded of her until the morning, when she heard quite clearly a sharp bark; short, and neutral enough.

A rhythm now settled in the house made up of predictable patterns of comings and goings through the snow; a muffled world in so many ways. Then the February rain and sleet began to rid them of this enclosing space and instead propelled people, bad-tempered, between one refuge to another from the biting winds. Anna ached to be doing things, conscious that the year of her widowhood was on her, and instinct told her she had had all the compassion she could expect. People's memories being very short. Life itself being very short.

The job came from an unlikely source via Louise from the solicitor who'd managed Louise's divorce.

'But your social life, yes, what can you do? I know, don't I know what it's like. I'm also on my own. Not like you, of course . . .'

Something else had become difficult for Anna: Dave had been acting oddly. Grateful for offers of help – and of company – she'd been in the habit of making coffee, offering a drink, listening to him talking (which he did at the drop of a hat), about his business which involved a good deal of wheeling and dealing and sounded less than honest. And he made her laugh. He'd helped with a stuck ball-cock, and recently unjammed the swollen back door. But he was a flirt. He even flirted with the children, including everyone in his expansive kingdom. Janet must have known her husband better than Anna so it was peculiar she should suddenly complain that Anna was always holding onto David and she could get nothing done for herself. Anna protested he never stayed very long. And after this both of them popped in and out of Anna's house on the slightest excuse, with Dave if anything appearing to encourage Janet to believe that he lingered on in Anna's house. It had made an awkwardness between them.

'Well if one of my friends' husbands fancies me – '

'He does *not* fancy me.'

'If I need a bit of help with something, I string them along to get the job done.' So said Louise, trying, as she said, to be realistic and practical, which Anna must learn to be.

It was not so easy for Anna as the men were afraid she'd weep on their shoulders, which she had done.

'I cry as well.'

'They're *different* sorts of tears, Louise.'

'What about your lodger. Can't he help do anything?'

Anna began laughing. Lord no. Helpless as a babe. In fact his passivity in front of the many domestic breakdowns incurred in this dreadful winter continued to exasperate her.

Louise had heard Japanese men were pampered. But the important thing: was he safe to leave the children with? 'Do you trust him? Because I was going to suggest a cinema. When was the last time you went out?'

The evening with Louise was only a moderate success. Louise herself was so liberated by her freedom that she lived in a continual state of euphoria which showed in every action, and Anna was soon conscious of this as she tried to keep up with Louise exuberantly walking through the West End, striding in her boots, her coat in spite of the cold swinging open, and saw the looks directed at them, specifically at Louise, from both men and women. She certainly looked on top of the world. Anna told her so.

'I'm my own woman now. And I love it. If one's confident, things fall into your lap. Try it and see. People fall over like ninepins if you believe in yourself. Believe me.'

'Oh I believe you.'

31

Louise put out her hand warmly, grasping Anna's. 'Things will get better. You're young. And you're managing so well. But you need some help with that money. You should get an accountant.'

'We never had . . . I don't think I want . . . '

'Michael might do.' Louise crinkled her eyes – that was new too. 'Let's have one last drink. It gives me courage, having to go home at night alone. What's he really like, your lodger?'

'Hard to say. Clean, neat, but no personality, really. Nothing that shows. He's never cross, or elated, or annoyed. Just polite . . . except for the awful way he eats. When I come to think of it, there are quite a number of places where I don't understand him at all; where he does things upside down, I suppose you'd say. I don't take much notice of him.'

Taking the papers to a client for John Summers involved Anna in a train-ride into the Kent countryside. There and back would take her into the evening, when she could collect the children from Janet. Movement helped sort out her thoughts. Her ignorance of ordinary affairs scared her. She'd better get wise. There's just yourself; no neighbour, no friend can help in the end. This advice to herself coincided with the stop before her station. Anna jerked herself out of introspection, for an old woman was trying to get into the carriage, the door was pushing against her arm. Anna felt the heavy weight swing away easily from her as she helped the woman in, who sank back breathless, gave a little nervous smile, and immediately turned away, fidgeting in her bag for privacy. Anna's thought winged back to that previous week when the vicar had introduced her at a club for widows. We understand you're not ready yet, he'd said after Anna had fled. He was right. But not in the way it seemed. Aghast, that was the word. Walking in, she'd been confronted with twenty ageing faces. Patient, warm, kind and friendly, they'd looked up, trying to welcome. All of her shouted no. No, she was not ready as she had been only up to two months ago to be put to one side. So get on with it, she said as she got down into the country town. She would consult this accountant; and she'd make that young man come out of his shell. And surely it was warmer?

Michael Boston had a nice sense of humour, and made even a sandwich at a pub a pleasant sensation. He told her several places to make savings and drafted a haughty letter to the Tax Authorities between the beer mugs.

'I don't think I can afford you.'

'Worry about that later.'

'I'm worried about it now. I'm an ordinary person, I can't go in for fancy stuff.'

To entertain him, for so little went on in her life and he'd told her about his dog, she told him about the fox and the amusing way the neighbourhood had been so agitated by its howls.

'It must have been a vixen, I think. Mating call. Ghastly sound.'

'Probably, but I still think of it as a fox. Hideo was very concerned about it.' And she told him about Hideo. Had Michael ever met any Japanese?

He'd a businessman as a client, as a matter of fact. But he was not someone one could get to know. There was nothing to say about most of his clients. In fact, she sounded far from ordinary to him with her Japanese lodger and her wild fox in the night.

It was nice to be teased. But nothing much happened to her.

'Except being widowed.'

And she liked his straightforwardness, turning her head, catching as she did so the comforting smells of pub food, and beer mingled with wood smoke which the cold winds blew every now and again back down into the room. Louise had recommended him and no doubt for his practical good sense. It was ironic that meeting him she'd been made more than ever concerned about how to make ends meet. But she knew that the bereaved, like the ill, are an embarrassment, if they go on talking.

'Look. I'll come round one evening. It shouldn't take long to go through the papers. Provided you let me smoke? All right. Louise asked me. I'm fond of Louise. Okay?'

Walking together as a couple to the door was a bad moment for Anna. At the door she thanked him. Her father had suggested as a solution that she should sell and all move back. No one could want this if there was the slightest chance of keeping her own home. That thought removed the traces of self-pity (that wretched emotion again) that had followed her out with the smell of the beer.

The winter had shown its beautiful face; day after dreary day it now showed ill-temper. A sharp cutting wind and sleet forced the head down so that neighbours missed each other in the street; and the other scourge of winter, the fevers and aches, started to sneak into households. Small things enraged Anna: Nick had lost his gloves. Right, she'd warned him. Another delivery of documents had left her fretful when the train was delayed with frozen points; now she sat down to knit mittens.

'I won't,' Nick said with some heat. They were babyish, he'd rather get cold, he would not, he'd lose them deliberately.

34

Anna tried the voice of good-humoured reasonableness, she tried the firm voice, she had been jovial, she left the subject alone for some hours, but just before bedtime she'd insisted as the weather report warned of further cold. Fay unwisely took her mother's side, Nick refused, so Anna hit him. It was at this moment that Hideo returned.

One expected him to leave in embarrassment at the sight of a furious little boy, shouting, tears running down his face, hands clenched, but he did not. He looked over at Nick, almost (but not quite) ignoring Anna.

'You have big trouber,' he asked in compassion, 'bery big trouber?'

The fury in Anna vanished. Fay, her arm round Nick's shoulder, held out the offending objects. 'They're Nick's gloves.'

Hideo said Ah, slowly, perhaps as he considered the near impossibility of pronouncing 'glove'. 'They bery good.' It was not possible for Nick to stay miserable. 'They're mittens,' he said, to make the distinction clear to this new ally.

Hideo's face lightened with exaggerated pleasure and joy. Ah, mittens, and he studied them with every sign of interest. It was like being hit smartly on one's funny bone to hear him repeat the word as if it was new and important, asking Nick to write it down. Nick glanced swiftly over at his mother, lowered his eyes and muttered: these were mittens because they had no fingers. Gloves had fingers. Anna left; she couldn't cope.

When she returned, Hideo was kneeling before the coffee table. He was folding paper into birds; no one looked up. (Even the kitten sat, its paws neatly folded together, eyes bright, fascinated.) Absorbed, his fingers folded calmly, and deftly turned the flat into solid. His head bent towards her had hair which was almost blue-black and densely shining. Fay was right about his colouring, but what suddenly caught Anna was the perfection of his skin; smooth, in the light of the lamp it was without flaw. He must have felt her study for

35

he looked quickly up, gave a small inclination of the head, gravely passing another bird he had made. 'Nick happy now.'

'What did you do today?' she asked in gratitude for the sympathy he'd shown, for now it was over she knew how she dreaded confrontations with the children, so afraid she was of losing them.

'I go to Rondon to meet some men.'

Anna bowed her head over the paper bird, for at his smile her heart seemed to have risen into her throat and she couldn't understand herself. Nick's voice was anxious. 'It's a crane, see?' The wings of the bird tipped up, optimistic.

Fay down beside him, her legs tucked like his under her thighs, was trying to fold some of his fine white paper. 'I go Karairu house,' he said slowly.

Where?

He repeated the name, the children shrugged, Anna said doubtfully she didn't think . . .

'Writer. Big man.'

'Karairu? That's not an Englishman.' Shaking her head, Anna thought she could detect a dimming in his eyes, surely not disappointment, and the children got to their feet sensing something was finished, for the time being. He rose too. I go work, leaving Anna on her own. But then to her astonishment he stood formally to say in some severity: 'Nick, he bery smarru boy,' as if rebuking her. What had she done?

In the night such a cold wind blew that for the first time she could remember the windows were written over with the fern shapes of frost. The cherry tree which she and Gregory had planted when newly married, stood isolated at the back of the garden, its trunk black, and a lacy line of hoar along the branches. The wind instead of lessening was getting more fierce and swirled up the road carrying fresh snow with it. In the garden the snow, powdery and very fine, lay deeper than the previous fall. The birds were silent. This morning there came another call from Tokyo. Hideo was coming down the stairs heavily clad as Anna held out the phone, and he shook his hands in the curious way which she took as meaning no. For a moment as they looked at each other, his skin warm and golden in the blue cold light of the hall (hello, came the soft voice, this is Tokyo), she thought he wavered. But he walked past, and she could then say accurately enough that he was not there. But his action was unintelligible. She could make nothing of it.

For days the weather was bad. The children stayed away from school; they asked about the fox. Was there shelter beyond the trees? A swoop of wind was playing with the snow, whipping it round in eddies, pulling it upwards into a point before dropping it to one side. The fences bent and swayed, but sometime in the night the snow had frozen onto the branches so that the bamboo, weighted down, was now bent over into hoops and fixed to the ground. The sky was a thin menacing grey. It was impossible to get warm.

'The telephone is out of order.'

'Ahhh?'

'The telephone does not work. It will be some days before they can put it right.'

'Ah, *so*, *desu* . . . ' Hideo appeared pleased. But she could not be sure of him. Returning one day, her head throbbing from cold, she was jolted on walking into what she assumed was an empty house to find him cross-legged on the floor and so silent in himself he gave no sign of hearing or seeing her. An hour later he had not moved. She went to her room and stood for a while, banished somehow, with the continuing east wind cutting its way through the weak joints in the windows, chilling her fingers. Cross with him, she took some tea nevertheless, and peered with a small uneasy smile into his

37

face. His eyes were an almond shape, their edges clearly pronounced as if folded over, they were, far more than the western face, like openings into depth; curiously this, together with his smooth creaseless skin made the face more, not less of a mask. There was not a flicker of expression. Then the blackness of the eyes somehow diluted and he bent slightly, placing his hands round the cup, ignoring the handle. He said nothing at all, and an inner cold gripped her near her heart.

'Anna! Anna how are you coping? We've been so worried about you.'

Her parents. They'd had drifts halfway up their lane, never known a winter like it, and one of them far from well, they'd thought how could a doctor, but anyway enough of that, things improve gradually (her father said), they'd got really concerned when they found they couldn't get her by phone. One thing, one comfort, was knowing there was a young man in the house.

Anna laughed.

'But that's awful. Surely you ask him to clear snow at the least?'

'He's completely useless. In fact he's worse than that. He nearly set fire to the kitchen.' Hideo had tried to make some of that peculiar soup; the whole pan and miso had fused together into a black mass, smoke had filled the house, the kitten fled in panic into the snow, and was now poorly, so one thing led to another. Easier to do things herself.

'Don't do too much for him and spoil him, that would be an unkindness. When in Rome, you know . . .' There was a pause. 'I'm pleased you can laugh about it. He sounds far too much trouble. And how are *you*?' he asked gently.

How was she. She was coping. She couldn't tell how Gregory had defaulted on tax, and bills. The full implications were only now coming to her; thinking only of getting through one day at a time, and then one week at a time, she'd forgotten that the world outside plans ahead in months and years. If she was not to be submerged, or forgotten or elbowed aside, she had to get things in order.

'If they find out about this lodger, you'll queer your pitch, you know that? These papers really are an awful mess.' Michael sighed from the edge of the couch, kind eyes and a gentle mouth. Hideo had refused to join them.

'Oh, I'm sorry.' She turned her back on the papers.

He grimaced. 'Sorry I have to come again? Thanks.'

'Of course I didn't mean that. You have been so kind. I would never have asked for myself, but it's the children. I love my children. I think I always loved them more. They're all I have.' Anna knew how fierce she must sound. 'I'll fight tooth and nail – '

'It won't come to that, I hope. And don't apologize. I enjoy being here.'

The journey from the centre of the room to its edges had taken away the effects of the whisky they were drinking, and she accepted some more, aware of an anguish, perhaps a feeling of fright, and then within seconds there she was, giggling, telling stories. For some reason she always felt she had to amuse him.

'Has Louise told you anything about me?' he asked suddenly.

'Not much.'

'I was crazy about her.'

'Ah.'

'Well, we still are very fond of each other.'

Oh dear, he wanted to talk about Louise and his relationship with her; in the past she would have been full of curiosity, but now it struck her that she didn't want to know. She frowned into her drink.

'I see. That's very loyal of you.'

'Heavens, it's not that.' She didn't want to pay the price of listening to confidences. But, she considered ruefully, one always has to pay, one way or another. But he misinterpreted her tapping fingers. 'Now you're cross with me. You lose your temper quickly?'

'Why should I do that?' wanting very much to be on her own, her nerves for some reason jangling.

'Your red hair, I suppose.'

Inside herself Anna groaned. Did he really mean this? And yet he was a nice man, yes, surely nice. She refused more whisky, he took some, and on her beginning, 'Should you . . . ?' he said, 'How like a wife,' but bitterly, and put down the glass. Anna felt irritated. If all her new friendships were going to go like this . . . but to sit in horrid silence was against her instincts, she liked to get things out in the open. So she apologized for still retaining the habits of a wife, but really she'd only had in mind that the roads were treacherous. To herself she decided there was a tension in him which had nothing to do with her.

He must have come to some conclusion for he grew rapidly cheerful and, gathering papers together, asked for strong black coffee.

'My brothers used to tease me for the pleasure of watching me explode, and I exploited that because my mother always rescued me rather than endure the noise. My Japanese doesn't like argument at all. He was telling me off for standing up to Nick. What a cheek.'

'They're inscrutable, these Orientals.'

'Are they? It's just because we can't talk each other's language.'

'Same thing.'

Was it the same thing? Waiting by the curtains while Michael tried to get the car engine to turn over, now anxious in case he could not get going at all and would have to stay the night, Anna saw Dave and Janet returning from some evening out. They hesitated outside their house. Michael at last caught a flicker and the car roared into life, he hooted, the sound loud in the crisp air. Anna expected some response to her wave but neither Janet nor her husband gave it; they went slithering up the path to their door, leaving Anna staring out at the cold, hard night.

Would it continue like this for ever? The cold made them all quiet. Even the kitten slept more, its nose firmly clamped behind its paw, the ball of it so tight that Fay found it hard to burrow her fingers into its fur. The future looked as impenetrable and hostile as the skies. Anna longed to move, to travel; more than she had ever done. And Hideo was causing worry. He had a cold, refused to eat, and stayed shut in his room. The house became more oppressive than ever as she moved quieter and quieter, straining her ears for any sound. But then he'd suddenly pad down the stairs to the bathroom; there he would expectorate in a blood-chilling manner as if turning his lungs inside out. Standing outside his room asking if he needed anything, he never replied, and she gave up. She didn't know how he lived.

Janet no longer came. Oh the effort, said Louise on the phone; Anna didn't know how lucky she was to stay at home. Anna couldn't agree. Imprisoned in her house by circumstance, side by side with an inexplicable sense of yearning was the impression growing stronger that the ordinariness of

41

things was skewed. Malignant things brought by the biting east wind.

'It's five days and I can't do anything with him. Hasn't he a tutor or someone to watch over him?'

The Bursar after the pause she always seemed to allow whether on the phone or not, admitted that she was the one in that position: that somehow what with the many things she'd had to arrange vis-à-vis his stay, the fact that he hadn't a clear timetable like the others had led to her assuming the lot. It had not seemed he was in need of pastoral care . . . but in any case, a doctor, did Mrs Dean think? Or what? So unfortunate: the weather, different manners . . . had he had more telephone calls? She wished that the mothers of these rich children would leave them alone to grow up (clearly something that morning had got her on the raw). 'I'll leave him in your good hands. All he wants no doubt is a bit of mothering.'

Of course! Misled by that light high voice, why hadn't it occurred to her that it could be Hideo's mother who kept on ringing? The voice behind the voice? Anna went to Hideo's room, knocked and went boldly in. He was lying very straight on his back looking at the ceiling, and although there was a pile of used tissues he didn't seem to have tossed and turned with fever. His skin was more yellow, perhaps, but when she put a hand on his brow a flush showed. No, he was not hot. Passively he lay while she cleared round him; throwing out more sachets, Anna turned in query, but thought better of it. He gave a cough, she turned her back quickly, moved to the window and saw the fox at last.

The animal was standing boldly at the back of the garden facing the gap at the fence. Its muzzle was lifting as if to scent something, and one paw was poised ready to run, the full brush ending in a white tip that lost itself in the snow. But it was thin. The fox, in full daylight. Incredible! But Hideo had turned suddenly onto his side. 'Fox not good.'

'Why,' Anna said surprised, 'don't the Japanese like foxes?'

'*Hai*, yes.' he said. He pulled the sheet over his head.

In the garden as the daylight went, a bird against all the discouragement of the cold sang its song: a thin and sparse note with pauses, as tentative, Anna was thinking angrily, as herself. During the entire afternoon she had done nothing but household manoeuvres of one forgettable sort or other; now she had been asked to pop next door to look after their children while the parents were out. Was this going to be a future pattern? That people would assume she had nothing much to do, ever? It was true. Jealousy is a green emotion that curdles the stomach as hers was now; she was jealous of the married, the unscarred, and felt apart from them and their togetherness. She envied people to whom things happened, their trips, their weekends, the possibility of a fulfilled life. She could see Dorothy next door even now leaning forward towards the mirror as she was short-sighted, applying lipstick, displaying as she did so the new seamed tights she'd just told Anna about. One is forever touching one's legs, she'd said, to check the wretched things.

Wandering round Dorothy's later that evening, Anna felt still this doleful sense of being on the margins even of ordinary life, of being exiled somehow. She looked in now through the doorways at other ways of living, following the trail of Dorothy's perfume back to its bottle, absentmindedly putting the top back on, but taking in the slapdash nature of the house, rather like her own.

The night was very cold. Anna hesitated on the pavement, caught by a disinclination to go back inside, for even this small journey had felt like some kind of release. The sky was clear, the stars bright, and dense in a band she supposed was the Milky Way. The half moon lit the snow and threw shadows onto the frozen ridges of ice disguising the kerbs; the road was still a one-way track. It was a different land she stood in.

Letting herself into the house she found Fay sitting up; she hadn't wanted to go to bed. Someone had called. So late? A man, she said, and she hadn't seen him well because she'd hidden behind the door. He'd asked for Hideo? Well, what he'd said was did Hideo live here and she'd said yes. Was that all right? He hadn't said who he was. He hadn't said he'd return. And yes he might have been another Japanese, but he talked much better. Just like everyone else.

'Didn't you ask his name?'

'Of course I did. And he just laughed.'

Anna thought about this. 'You said Hideo was unwell? What a pity if a friend . . . No. He should have left a name. Or a card. They always carry cards.'

'Well I didn't like him coming when you weren't here. He kept ringing and ringing the bell and I had to get out of bed and I didn't like it.' She was beginning to cry.

'Sorry, pet,' Anna said. 'I'm here. You're safe.'

In the night they were woken again by the cry of the fox.

'How old did you say he was?'

'He must be about twenty-four or so.'

'He's a grown man then. You can't make him do anything.'

'But it's a week! If he was ill I wouldn't mind. But I don't believe he is.'

Her brother hated the cold and always tried to stay in bed, didn't Anna remember? 'You mustn't get too involved over this, Anna. We'll be over as soon as it's possible to drive safely for your father. It is so beautiful out here in the country, but have you heard how the animals are dying?'

44

And of course humans are far more important. Anna gave herself a shake. The cold affected one's spirits. It was ridiculous to allow oneself to be influenced by it.

And now, Fate playing into her hands. 'Hideo,' she called up. 'You *must* come down. It will make you feel better.'

There was to be a series about Japan, about which the English were supposed to be in total ignorance; so its history, its people, its meteoric rise in world importance were going to be explained, illustrated, discussed and analysed over several weeks. Hideo sat passively by her side in his sleeping suit; Nick and Fay lay on their stomachs at their feet where they quickly became entranced, and Anna forgot herself in images of exquisiteness. For the first time in many months the walls of her room disappeared. As image after image filled her mind she accumulated a sense of softness, of delicacy and a refined quiet, of women merged from painting into flesh with gestures that were gentle and contained. Their fingers fluttered delicately over zithers, or made refined movements in the tea ceremony. Such lovely creatures, even though the geisha with her chalk-white skin and astonished eyebrows did look ridiculous clacking to an appointment where she performed music of real painfulness, breaking the spell, and waking Anna up.

There, her eyes sparkling. Didn't he enjoy that?

'Bery beautifu.' He said it dutifully and appeared bored by it all. It had ravished Anna, so that if she closed her eyes she could see again the red pillars of palaces, the golden slit-eyed Buddhas. But he was unimpressed even by her enthusiasm. He nodded politely, and padded back upstairs.

Going past the mirror in the hall, Anna could not help glancing. The images of dainty ladies were with her still. She found herself gross. Too big, too tall, her face heavy, her nose far too large for her face. For a minute or so she could see how she must appear to a Japanese: that her eyes would seem bulbous and staring, her mouth wide and too full of teeth. What a joke. Her smile she could see was positively frightening, and her loud cheerful gestures like some large animal

45

blundering around. No wonder this young man had taken to his bed. It was like being banished to a land of goblins. Anna grimaced into the mirror. Gradually the uncouth features faded back into her familiar face. But the impression of ugliness took far longer to go away.

The programme had one good effect: Hideo went back to college. Going to change his sheets she found the room in order. The effort of the entire week was on the table. In neat script he had written: 'I am in England. My mother is very kind; she does ikebana. My father is very stern; he plays golf. I have no brother or sister.' The pencils and pens were laid out as before, but what was new and more concerning was the addition of a knife which Anna took to be for cutting paper until she saw it could not possibly be. And it was far too sharp.

That dreadful morning, bitterly cold, Anna had run down-stairs, having woken late, in bare feet to get the kettle boiling quickly before the children should come down. The first thing in the darkened kitchen was her foot slipping on something unpleasantly lumpy and wet, and she lost her balance and slid into the table. With the light on she saw the carnage but could not believe it, could not recognize, so far it was from anything she could have thought. As she stared first at her feet, at the skid of blood, and then at the torn bits lying all over the kitchen, her mind spun round trying to get some hold while she at the same time fought with the feeling that she was going to be dreadfully sick. For the kitten had been savaged; torn literally apart. Hearing a sound behind her she turned violently to shut the door in the face of any child, action bringing her strength. But it was Hideo. He shut the door fast behind him, leaning against it. Quickly, she said, the children . . .

46

Afterwards she would remember that he grew up before her eyes, moving with a surprising swiftness. As Anna swayed, holding a bag she'd brought him he picked up the pieces of the kitten with his bare hands and afterwards took the bag outside. Anna was beginning to weep, when the realization that she had to do something about the children came home to her. Appalled by this she stopped and washed the floor in a kind of blank despair. For they loved it; it had taken them through those first bad months after their father's death; she could hear their agonized voices asking, Why, as children will. But as she automatically moved to the kettle she knew another story would have to be made.

When Nick and Fay came into the room exactly as usual, Anna didn't need reminding that innocence is often a lack of knowledge, and that one only knows it is a state of bliss when it has been lost. She was trembling and felt polluted, noticing how easy it proved to lie and say she had a cold, seeing by their quietness that they were not completely taken in, sensing something, noticing a smell, but sufficiently reassured to eat. Hideo stood by the back door, his hand on the lock. 'The snow goes, I think,' he said gravely. 'The spring comes.' Fay glanced over with a smile meaning to convey: He's talking! but Anna found the smile she tried to send back check halfway. Where's the kitten? they'd asked casually as they wrapped into coats, as she knew they would, accepting that it was somewhere around.

Fox, Hideo said when they'd gone, still showing that calm acceptance as if this was in the nature of things. There could be no other explanation, and when one looked closer at the cat-flap the door panel was loosened, and come open; the cold perhaps had dried and shrunk the wood in an old door; and it had been home-made by Gregory for the first animal they'd had. But she'd also apparently forgotten to lock the door. She thought she'd done it, but Hideo said not. So she was in some sense responsible. It had not even been closed. A rank smell brought out by the warming air hung near the door. Outside the ground was rock-hard, showing no marks of feet. It would be impossible to bury the remains.

Anna knew the stages they would have to go through: the questions, the unhappiness, the blame. After talking with her father she decided, and trying to explain to Hideo found it too complicated. She was going to say that the kitten, which had been sleeping a lot, had some illness, she'd taken it to the vet and he was keeping it. The following day she would follow this warning, by telling them it had to be put down.

'You tell them it was fox.'

'Oh no. I can't do that. It is too cruel.'

'But it is the animal way.'

But she wasn't sure. She'd never heard of anything like this, but the winter was exceptional and so . . . 'We say nothing about the fox.' He didn't understand.

When he returned in the evening their eyes met and he gave an almost imperceptible nod. Once the children were in bed he came down – unusual for him these days. He had something to show her.

It was a line drawing showing a group of peasants lying in a field, drunk. Sitting with them were several women who were not drunk at all, although something was intoxicating them, but Anna had to look for some time before she saw it was a sense of great mischief which was transforming their looks. One had the hindquarters of an animal showing beneath her kimono, the others had features subtly changing, while from behind the fan of another woman cradling a man's snoring head in her silky lap, peered the grinning face of a fox. It was frankly erotic.

'Ah. Yes. I see.' But she didn't see at all. When he had come into the kitchen that morning they had looked at each other, and there had been no need, thank God, for once, for words. What now was he trying to make her understand? She could feel a weak little smile of bafflement coming once more onto her face. He also was frustrated, for he banged the top of his head . . . over and over again.

48

The thaw came suddenly towards the weekend, bringing Anna's father through flood waters to collect the children and keep them till Monday. What a terrible thing to happen to them. He moved swiftly round the subdued children, anxious to be away and back before dark. The things that had happened this winter were quite unprecedented, he said angrily, as if he sought someone to blame. Left alone, Anna found the house intolerable; perhaps others had felt imprisoned by the snow, for the streets were crammed as she went to the town.

Something was happening to her, as if under the influence of a malign spell, for although she'd seen several neighbours and they'd greeted her as if her face showed normal, inside she was seething from a sort of fury, looking in disgust at tat from every quarter of the world, primped up, polished and in its party clothes beckoning with come-on looks from every counter. In a book shop (a jostling damp crowd) it was the same – more elevated but still keen to buy itself presents – and Anna succumbing in front of a bank of paperbacks wanted to buy herself a present too. But within the frame of the book was the same grab for attention: eyes, lips, breasts and thighs competed with battleships, country kitchens, palm trees and skulls. She rejected them all and picked a book of soft faded colours, the drawing a crazy perspective.

For the rest of the day Anna read. She forgot to eat, sunk so deeply into the daily life of this sharp observer in tenth-century Japan, the Lady Shonagon. Sometimes she laughed out loud, lifting her head with a long sigh to find she'd finished and it was dark.

'By the way, so sorry, but do you make food?'

49

In front of her were other books about the enigmatic world that was his home. She pointed in her turn at a picture of men dressed as samurai, as bizarre a collection as science fiction.

Hideo peered politely. 'Ahhh . . . samurai. Bery good fun. Maybe.'

The samurai costume with helmets winged like cock-chafers were as interesting to him as the Changing of the Guard to her, perhaps, but as he turned to leave she quickly called him back: she mustn't be left alone, she'd go mad alone. 'Let's go out.'

A hasty decision; and now he'd adopted that apathetic pose again, standing to one side, waiting. What did he want to drink? going through some types while the landlord with an exaggerated flourish polished a glass. Hideo wouldn't say. Two lagers then, and food. Why couldn't the man walk with her and not pad behind as if hiding behind her back? They waited. A couple were trying, in an obvious manner, not to look in her direction. Anna always thought now in terms of the before and after time when Gregory had been the one to do things, the decision maker, the one to order . . . She tried to catch the landlord's eye – she was really getting desperately hungry but clearly there was something risible about Hideo sitting patiently beside her. The landlord just winked, and when the chicken-in-the-basket arrived there were chopsticks to eat with. Her colour rose, a laugh came from the bar as Hideo doubtfully lifted his chopsticks. 'Use your fingers, and be damned to them.' She ate, describing to Hideo what he apparently didn't know, the fascinating daily life of the thousand-year-old Lady Shonagon, so modern in her likes and dislikes. They relaxed. But not for long.

'Glory be, fancy seeing you here!' Jiggling money in his pocket, standing over them was Dave. Anna considered him good-looking in a fair, English way; a zappy dresser, wearing clothes a week before one saw them in the supplements. But something was awry with these neighbours. Dave was too jovial; early giving up all attempts to talk with Hideo, he

50

concentrated on Anna with occasional digs at his wife. Janet was not speaking. The episode of the kitten came back sickeningly but they were clearly not interested in why the children were away. 'Really! So you're by yourselves. Another round?' And Anna was asking herself how she'd seen Janet as a real friend. Was it just proximity that kept the relationship going? She was keeping up a bantering conversation in growing discomfort when the silent Janet's demeanour, which had also been sour, suddenly changed. Anna first of all glanced across the room. Many more people had come in, and the pub was a typical Saturday-night crowd; there was another neighbour who, being loudly dressed, could have caused Janet's change of mood. She was sitting now, looking straight ahead with a smile of malicious pleasure on her face. Anna didn't realize where the source was coming from until she followed Dave's look of amusement focused on Hideo, who was sitting neatly as always. But soft giggles were coming from him, and his face was alarmingly red. Then he began, with a winsome charm, to sing.

Dave offered to see them home, but Anna, furious and for whatever reason also ashamed, refused his help until she saw that the progress to the door, usually a matter of indifference to a Saturday drinking crowd, would this time be far more interesting, Hideo's way of not holding his drink being intriguingly watchable. But she adamantly refused Dave's help any further than her front door; she heard him walk smartly off down the path.

Once inside, she propped Hideo against the hall wall and they looked at each other.

'I have fun,' he said, taking care over every syllable.

'Good. I'm glad.' He'd certainly added to the pub's fun.

'We go back soon, in a minute.' A gentle crooning began in the back of his throat. He held an invisible microphone in his hand. But his world was very unstable for he was swaying gently against the wall, and her own was not too level either for she was not used to strong drink. 'Bed, Hideo.' His eyes

51

glinted, and the house, so quiet, hung around them expect-
antly.

'I think we both ought to go to bed,' she said, and then
cursed herself.

And he answered yes, and, 'Take me Ok'san.'

She kicked the shoes off her feet and gently propelled him
up the stairs; he was still singing in a quiet voice. Slowly they
made their way and at his door they stopped. Anna was by
this time such a mixture of reactions that she didn't want to
think any more, didn't even want to sleep any more: she was
desirous, she wanted to be loved, she wanted to be cared for,
and oh how she wanted to be understood, and she wanted to
be touched but that was the drink pleading. She opened the
door to lead him into the dark room when he flung his arms –
which were astonishingly strong – round her, making her
weak with longing at the feel of an adult human body, and
then . . . he broke out into loud theatrical sobs. A tired child.

A note in a book somewhere points out in what way silence is
important to the Japanese; how it is full for them, and not
vacant as so often for the peoples of the West. Anna's house
felt full, so tangibly silent that she shook that Sunday
morning when the telephone rang. Fool. It could only be her
father.

'This is Tokyo.'

'He is sleeping.'

The pause on the other end was so long that she began
making a construct of what might be being said; questioning
what was the time in London and whether it was right that
English people would be awake. 'Tell him we will ring again
in an hour.'

52

Hideo was standing behind her. They were the same height in bare feet and she could not think why she'd thought him short. The air was fresh, not cold, and the church bells were ringing crisply. He had no sign of a hangover, and there was to her great relief no sign of self-consciousness. It was she who was still abashed. There was a faint glow to his skin, his eyes that unfathomable black. 'We go to church, Mama San?'

Church?

Deliberately she'd sat at the back. It hadn't lasted long for with the psalms he began giving his head small shakes as if trying to dislodge an insect trapped in there.

Terribu.

He *had* to learn the *l* and the *v*, Anna said severely. He had caused some uncomfortable moments with a churchwarden and she didn't know where she was with him. Was he Buddhist then?

'I am Shinto.'

A very undemanding religion, Anna knew, having seen on the film the clap to arouse the gods, the bow, and the finishing clap of the hands as perfunctory a signal as sticking one's hands out of a car window.

'The land of the Rising Sun.'

'Yes, that is true.'

And did he know what she'd just found out, that Europe meant the land of the Setting Sun? He laughed gaily when she finally got him to understand, but the confident way he laughed chilled her. Was he saluting her wry humour, or happily agreeing with her that Europe was on the way out, with the new strong empire of the Pacific taking its place of influence?

How could they understand each other? Mere words were hard.

She said: 'The next film is about the samurai.'

Ah.

'So you will at least hear some Japanese spoken.'

Hideo smiled. 'I go study now.'

53

The promised telephone call hadn't come; or had it been while they were in church? Quick thinking on Hideo's part? And had it been that gentle mother who did ikebana? The voice she had eavesdropped was anything but soft, not to her ears. It had been shrill, the tone hysterical, surely. In any case disquieting. From the window, the only snow left was a sordid heap with bits of twigs sticking in it. It was already hard to think back to the weeks ago when she had stood at the door. Now the outside world was at long last modifying gently, waiting to shape into spring.

'I really do wonder, Anna,' her father was saying when they arrived back that Sunday afternoon. (The difference in the weather, the alteration in Hideo made it seem far more than the few days since the attack.) He stood with his back to her, a sign of embarrassment, disquiet or something. 'I question about that fox. I've never heard of such a thing happening before, but I suppose it's the only explanation. The world can be very disturbing at times. When you really have no reason to expect it, I mean. But you've been managing so well, and . . . ' he turned round, ' . . . the children are better for the change with us. They've had some harsh lessons to learn about life. What about a dog for them? It might be a protection for you.'

'We don't need protection, Father, not here. Safe as houses.'

'Don't be over-confident. There's far more burglary, and you haven't a man in the house.'

'I have a man in the house.'

'Hardly. How's he behaving himself?'

'Typical Japanese. A model of decorum,' she lied hastily, 'except when he eats. And I'll think about the dog,' as he was leaving, 'but I know it will end up with me taking if for all the walks.'

*

One day Anna caught up with one of Louise's only free evenings for weeks. 'Michael *talks* about you,' Louise moaned; her tone deceptively bland. 'You've impressed him.'

'He's been very kind.'

'He wouldn't have been unless he really liked you, Anna.'

Louise had that kind of gleam on her, the gloss that constant polishing gives to objects; this minute attention to the details of her person was more noticeable now than at any time Anna had known her. Though why, when this was so impressive – her well-cut hair, her neat little nails, her eyes made up with precise lines of blue – should Anna think of the forced clipping and trimming of the bonsai tree?

Louise, upset by the fate of the kitten (and telling it had brought tears to Anna), shuddered openly, and took a long sip of her coffee. 'What do you *do* . . . ?' she began, and, 'Well you don't do anything, but it almost makes one believe in fate. What I mean is, even when we were younger the strange things always happened to you. We used to think you made things up. But if ever I had to hear of someone having something a bit out of the usual run happen to them, then I think of you. Perhaps,' she said brightly, 'there's compensations: splendid things happen as well.'

A memory came to Anna of Gregory, and Louise's ex-husband Daniel, drawing out some project or other on a table-napkin while Louise chattered to Anna in her clear laughing voice. Gregory could cut out everything when he was involved intellectually, but Daniel, who clearly could not, had frowned – it was the beginning of their break-up – irritated by that carrying sound.

'This whole winter everything has been out of the ordinary. Yes. It was very upsetting, but the death of an animal . . . it can't compare.'

'Oh Anna.'

She took a breath, and went on recklessly, asking about Michael.

'He's divorced as you know, little girl he sees at the weekends, very kind, very knowledgeable about lots of things. Maybe,' she added, checking on the side profile of one of her nails, 'a *bit* predictable, a bit boring sometimes?'

'Like me,' Anna said, regretting it instantly.

Returning home, short of breath, the clouds of it preceding her along the road in the night air, she could see some way before she reached it that her house had all the lights on, and going in at past eleven o'clock there was Fay. She was sitting watching a highly unsuitable film; she had been crying.

A nightmare? Fay had never been particularly afraid of the dark; she'd promised to turn off lights before they went up. She and Nick were quite happy to stay with Hideo: they hoped to get him to teach more origami. The attempt was on the coffee table.

Fay, leaning inside the curve of Anna's arm, told of another man who had called for Hideo. And someone had rung earlier too.

But he hadn't gone out after he promised to stay in?

He'd gone to do his work.

So?

So she'd done the lights and seen to Nick only he made a fuss, and the bell had rung and there was another man there, a Japanese man.

56

Same as last time?

'No. His voice was different. He was short. And sort of chuckly.'

Anna was confused. 'But did he frighten you?'

She whispered yes.

'How? How did he frighten you? What did he do?'

But Fay either couldn't or wouldn't say. She'd sat up putting all the lights back on, because she was afraid to go to bed. But what of Hideo in all this, after she'd shut the door? She'd gone to his room, he hadn't answered, so perhaps was asleep and she didn't know what to say. She sat twisting Anna's handkerchief into a sodden little lump and biting on the corners.

Silly one, Anna had said, but by herself she asked why it had happened that the only two times she had been out recently the men had come to the house. A coincidence, it must be.

'Last night a man came to the house for you. Thank you for looking after the children.'

'They are nice children.'

'Were you asleep when Fay knocked at your door?'

'Maybe.' His almond eyes were untroubled, as always.

'She's only ten years old, she feels the responsibility looking after the house, and she can't ask you anything complicated because you wouldn't understand, would you? This man worried her. I mean, do you understand what I'm getting at?'

'*Hai*,' he said uncertainly.

'Do you know who they are?'

'I do not think so.'

'We'll have to wait and see then.' She was losing her temper.

'I think so.'

Anna saw again the collected way he had gathered the pieces of kitten in his bare hands. Someone with that amount of coolness ought to be reassuring to have around. It was a question of language only. They are a different people, the

57

Japanese; they have a different way of looking at life; and if there are these differing ways of approach, whether to begin a book from the front or the back (so to speak), who is to say that one way is better than the other? And when it comes to understanding, Anna thought, remembering how Gregory continued to be an enigma even after his death, how can one know anything?

That on the surface settled the matter. So it appeared. But in her sleep she dreamt of foxes.

And only a few days after this, again something gently undermining. He'd stopped her, holding out his phrase book open at the medical section, Anna very conscious of his fine hands, fingers moving down the page. Next to his her hands were unpleasantly pink; she took them away ashamed. He was pointing with his finger to the phrase 'I have a headache', and then pointed at Anna. The Japanese script opposite was in red.

'Me? Do you mean because of those men? That's too strong.' There was nothing in the medical section that could in any way cover what she felt, and the choice was poor. She laughed, underlining the signs opposite 'I have palpitations', and he smiled, scanned the page and showed her the reply to that: 'If you don't feel better come and see me again.' It was a silly game.

'He is trying, of course, but I wish he got on faster with talking.'

'Oh,' Fay said, offhand, eating her tea and reading at the same time, 'he's getting quite good.'

'He talks all the time,' Nick said, 'and it's *me* that got him to say *l* properly.'

'You mean,' Anna asked slowly, 'that he talks more to you when I'm not around?'

Oh yes. Yes of course.

Why of course?

They laughed, they found it funny. 'He's too polite with you.'

Indeed. She was being made a fool of.

It was becoming clear that neither the children nor Hideo much liked Michael. The children were tiresome, and Hideo avoided him. And Anna had to admit that their friendship was not honest: he had his private reasons for seeing and helping her; she found him a support and reassurance over her fears about money. They met for the wrong reasons. Then one day she realized that the spring had stolen up on her. There was this lift to the air; it felt gentle on the skin, a few days later in the top right corner of her bedroom came soft scratching sounds which meant the sparrows were building again in the guttering. There had been a nest there before Gregory died, who'd liked birds.

At night she had the strongest impression of the entire garden of plants stretching and expanding in the moonlight. Here she waited, trying to penetrate the dark recesses at the end near the fence, in case some movement, or the giveaway white tip of the brush should show. There was no sign. The animal had retreated back, no longer driven, gone to earth.

Anna had been clearing away dead wood, things gone permanently through cold. 'If the bees are not all dead we shall have cherries.' The children were searching for the primroses they had helped their father plant, which they found in thick clumps of white arabis, but there were still empty spaces, and plants discouraged and feeble, unable to pull away from the effect of winter. Hot sun would kill them off. But Anna had never been so grateful for the coming of Spring. Hideo was looking round with real pleasure and, asked to pick the flower he liked best, he pointed without hesitation, choosing dandelion.

'They're called wet-the-bed,' Fay said, very quick.

'Really?' He laughed. '*Tampopo.*' He laughed and the children giggled. So . . . he understood.

In front of the mirror that night, slowly stroke by stroke the mother brushed the daughter's hair, and then slipping her arms over the thin shoulders linked fingers. There, you're trapped.

Fay's eyes dark in the lamplight met Anna's in the mirror; her eyes surveyed their figures in an appraising way.

'I might grow to be quite beautiful.'

'Of course.'

The child's eyes met the mother's eyes. In that light they were the same.

'He understands very well.'

The samurai came rushing through the village, swords already drawn. They ran swiftly. With rapid steps, stocky men, short-limbed, they jumped before they lunged, using the weight of the body falling to give extra thrust. The swords were sharp and ripped upwards viciously through the man's armour; he died horribly and at length, trying to remake his stomach. This fight was by way of preparation for further beastliness, a catalogue of horrors. Hideo was leaning forward in intense interest. Anna felt sick. The children had been put off at the beginning by the preamble about the samurai code of honour. Hideo grinned with an expression of keener enjoyment than they'd seen from him. 'It's good, like Western,' but the onset of part two devoted to the samurai ethical system got him hastily to his feet. He had discovered the joys of showering. But Anna remained, caught by the direct contrast with the previous week where it had been softness and aesthetic refinement. This code seemed to call for the highest degree of selflessness, quite admirable but at the present time what was the man suggesting? The samurai class had entered into the professions, and some part of the code was taken as a rule of conduct even by gangsters. The film cut abruptly to a startling clip of men in dark suits, respectably turned out, square confident men yet with something indefinable; and one of them good-looking, giving an idea of how Hideo would be older, and what was the man saying about them . . . ? She turned her head at the sound of splashing water, and when she turned back to the screen, the picture had changed, the point gone.

As it will, the sun released the energy pent up by the sinister winter, Anna not fully realizing the extent of the siege until these messages from the outside world started to come into the house. This morning brought several letters, one from her sister in Scotland suggesting a barge holiday if only someone else would do all the arranging; there was to be a party that Saturday at Dave and Janet's (the first invitation she'd received for a year); a discouraging letter from Michael about that tax; and an envelope also posted from the City which Anna at first didn't want to open. Buff, business envelope, official looking, it could only be a bill. Yet it was not a bill. It was a newspaper cutting. Which Anna read, and reread.

The cherry tree framed by the window glowed with pink-tinged whiteness. She pushed the sash window up. A teasing soft wind blew through, and pieces of the old newspaper padding fell to the floor and lay at her feet. This seemed significant enough. She put all the pieces into the bin.

She rang round her friends and made plans for meeting. She rang Louise. But Louise was not available. She rang Michael and it was he who told her why Louise was proving so hard to contact: she was away for the obvious reason that she was in love again; hardly went near her flat. This hurt. Louise must have known the man when they last met, she had said nothing. Well, Michael said uneasily, he would suppose Louise felt it tactless to go on about it.

'What did she think I'd do? Howl on her shoulder from jealousy?'

Probably.

Admit they might be right. 'Another thing, I've had this queer letter. It's a newspaper cutting. Just that. Nothing else. About a Chinese woman and her two children who were murdered in their home not far from here.'

Michael carefully said he didn't think it much of a joke. Perhaps some silly kid.

'From the City? I know no one in the City but you.'

He was quickly defensive. 'Well it wasn't me.'

'Not for a minute, but it's a bit weird.'

'There are weird people about.' He said it as a cliché. 'Do you want me to come over? I'm a bit stuck this week.'

'I'll ignore it. I'm fine.' She had to cope. 'I'll ignore it like obscene telephone calls.'

'Do you get those as well?'

'I don't. But talking of telephone calls – '

'Tell me next week.'

There had been no more calls from Tokyo. Hideo never asked to ring.

The day beginning like this became one of short shocks. It had become a habit with Anna to see what Hideo had written in his childlike hand. It was a way of getting to know more about him, because the language he used with her was still so elementary. 'I like England. I am going to Leicester Square,' he'd written the previous week, and as a supplement she had tried using the same phrases, hoping it would help. 'The dandelion is like a chrysanthemum. There is a cherry tree like the trees in Kyoto; they make us sad because the blossom does not last.'

Today the next set of phrases were written out because she could see the exercise book underneath, but what was on top was the Japanese version of *Playboy* open at a very open nude; he was also trying to find out more useful words as he'd written over the margins. It was obvious he meant her to see

62

this and something cringed inside her. She forced herself to look coolly at the big-bosomed pouting Occidental blonde, and realized what was odd about her: she was as smooth as a baby, with no body hair.

Anna cleaned the room. This was her income, but while she wiped round the basin she swept his washing things pettishly aside and left them.

Janet she saw by the shops loading quantities of bottles of drink into the car on the opposite side of the road. Cursing foreigners and in a mood to be friendly, Anna waved and called she was looking forward to the party.

'Bringing your Jap?' came the yell across the road.

Jap, like a slap. Clearly nothing had improved. Anna shook her head, smiling (she'd go on smiling on principle). He has his own life. But a kind of dull anger was taking her over; of course he had his own life, and it was foolish and short-sighted to allow herself to get involved. Things were going to improve now it was spring, and the glimpses into his world had tantalized, that was all, due to those sad days of winter. The shopping basket was heavier than usual, and she walked slowly back to the house. In the high April wind petals from the blossom were blowing in eddies in the road, leaving narrow drifts of clean petals on the grass, taking her mind back to the winter snow, so that it was both more and less of a shock to walk into the front garden and find two men on her doorstep.

Two of them, and clearly Oriental. She put down her basket, and put on a pleasant expression. Half expecting a bow she waited, but as if they were holding back for her to make the first move, they waited also. There was something unnerving about them, the way their arms hung down loosely in the dark city suits; the shoes were more flashy, one would say, than was correct with that dark cloth, and the cloth and the ties had a sheen about them that spoke a different taste. They're smart boys.

The study of their clothes was to stop her seeing their faces,

63

for one quick glance had been enough. One man was stocky, and thick in face and shoulders, hair cut razor-short, orientally unremarkable; but the other was taller than she knew now to expect, elegantly slender with well-shaped black hair, everything about him would have made him really handsome but for the appalling defect of his tiny eyes. These he kept fixed on Anna. Eventually she made herself look.

There was no movement in the man; this lack of reaction itself was remarkable. It alerted her.

'What do you want?' Instinctively she was on the defensive.

His eyes were tiny holes in his face. No eyelids, just the thin fold of skin; his eyes seemed all pupil, and no expression could be taken from them. Nor could one get anything from the smooth face, no lines showing frowns or smiles, yet something passed swiftly over his face. This one knew how to say his *l*s.

'We are calling for Hideo.'

'Have you called before? He's not in.'

'Why should we have done that?' There was no concession to the polite forms.

'Well someone called. Late, and without leaving any name. My daughter said someone.'

He turned to his companion. 'Who could that have been?' asking in English, then ignoring her he spoke in quick staccato Japanese. Anna reached down for her basket to get her key, changed her mind, the conference finished. Who should she say called? Perhaps they had cards?

'Friends. Some friends were asking for him.' His accent was somewhat American. 'Hideo is very popular.' His eyes hadn't left her face. The tone was light, and she felt she ought not to detect a sneer as he backed down the path, the other man having turned his back to walk away. Her heart was beating fast, and she was scared by the depth of her dislike. But once inside the house she scolded herself for not finding out more. She owed it to both Hideo and Fay to ask more questions. On

64

the other hand they were merely two visiting men, they
would see her as a landlady, and so unimportant; Hideo's
business was not her business . . . Nevertheless (as she
stacked away the groceries in the quiet house), they certainly
did not have that politeness, did they? And wandering around
the house to find a small task to do, she longed for something
to stroke, missing the kitten.

The little black dress; should she wear it or not? She smoothed
down the material with her hands, the silk unfamiliar after
all these months. Her skin white in the dusk; black made her
hair more red. She did not seem herself. Would some local wit
nickname her The Merry Widow? But no. For Dave had said
when he came round yet again to borrow something or other
that there would be hardly any other neighbours there, only
'favourites'. A relief to Anna, wishing to meet more people;
she was so tired of commiseration, feeling (and thinking it a
good sign for her) that she as a person was getting lost behind
her situation. But coming downstairs to ask the children their
opinion – a foolish weakness – she encountered Hideo coming
up. He swayed forward in a kind of bow. The unspoken
questions between them had accumulated during the last few
days, producing a high tension in Anna. The smooth luscious
image of that pouting blonde had constantly floated about,
inserting herself between Anna and her clothes, Anna and
her bath water, Anna and the bed . . .

'Beautiful.'

One could not take that for a compliment, considering that
the last time he'd used the word before her had been for a
dandelion. He was unmoved when told of visitors. For me?
What like? Well, one of them had small eyes . . . Ah,

Japanese eyes? Yes, that had been it. How to explain that her intuition had turned her against them? Especially when he said: 'They're friends. Not to worry.' A new phrase.

Her hand was sticky where she grasped the banister rail. 'There's another programme tonight,' looking down at him, 'about the Japanese family.' Did he want to watch, or was he – her voice was frosty – going to work at his books? Any European could have caught her tone. But no. He was going to Soho. Really?

They passed on the stairs. The first thing his eye would light on would be the open *Playboy*, plus new explicit vocabulary.

Hideo went out, trailing cologne. The children refused to watch the film; what on earth for, they said.

But Anna, with nothing more to do, and feeling her nerves wound tight, decided she was fated and might as well give in.

A woman, kneeling on a flat cushion. With a smile, and punctuating her remarks with little bows of respect to the camera, she was explaining the great honour of being a Japanese mother. The voice-over blotted out her voice, with strong Anglo-Saxon analysis: 'The Japanese child is the most indulged in the world. Until the age of six he holds undisputed sway. Between his mother and himself there is an almost suffocating bond. With the husband absent, as is customary, until late in the evening, the mother has complete power. She disciplines through love, her persuasion inexorably tender, for she has only these few years before the state takes the child to be moulded into the Japanese citizen. Never again will the individual know its uniqueness . . . '

Anna was paying close attention. The woman here was like her. Stuck at home. Almost, one could say, husbandless . . .

'Psychologists believe that the childishness displayed by the Japanese male, his seeking in groups the banal pleasures of the massage parlours, reveals the unresolved trauma of being taken from this indulged environment into the almost military style of schooling. No surprise then that some,

66

unable to take conflicting demands of adolescence, plus pressures of learning, succumb to feelings of worthlessness, and commit suicide.'

Food for thought. This was coming alarmingly close to home; Anna did not care for references to 'banal pleasures', and 'older women'. But the images shown with this depressing account were of children running, flying kites, clapping palms in front of a shrine where, in a telling shot the mother, kimono-clad and bound tightly round her middle, put out her hand and gently pressed behind the child's head to just the right angle for devotion.

'. . . And it is no surprise that some women without sufficient outlets for their talents become tyrants in their turn, employing cunning. The woman as vixen is familiar here.'

Anna did not know what to do with her speculations. She had no idea that such a combination of sinister charm could exist. Who were the women who rang? And who cared so much? And were his parents really people of such influence? "'My mother is kind; she does ikebana. My father is stern. He plays golf. I have no brothers or sisters.'"

They need not be inscrutable, but they must be different. And the moon even, she was thinking, getting up to see it shining over the garden and catching the whiteness of the blossom, they see as a man.

On Dave's doorstep Anna realized just how nervous she was; it was worse than being an adolescent. She had not been among such a crowd since Gregory's death and the first thing she noticed as she fought her way to a gin and tonic was that while she had been dealing with her ordinary life, dealing with illness, the world had moved on. And she did not recognize the house. What had they done to it? Surely it hadn't been newly decorated for a party? Furniture had been moved, or was gone completely. Everywhere the flickering light from candles made women's eyes large and voluptuous. In this light the dress made her too dramatic; even worse, when she moved it seemed to open up and slip on her shoulders, exposing her in a way she no longer liked. Everywhere she felt eyes appraising others, and her mind went back to the previous weeks when she had gone shopping. Some of the people here appeared from their predatory gleam to be after goods in the same way, searching, for experiences, for colour, for bargains. If she was honest with herself an element of this had to exist in her too; she did not want to be mateless for the rest of her life. Her fit of nerves was not improving – this in itself was discouraging, to be frightened at a party – and when at last she found Dave she grabbed him with more fervour than normal.

'Are they *all* friends?'

'All friends. My word, Anna, that dress. It's lovely to see you coming out of yourself! Where's your fella? Janet said you were bringing that – '

'I *told* Janet – '

'I'll fix you up. We'll get together later, you and I. Who deserves you, do you think? Clive!'

'Present and correct, skipper.'

'This is the delectable Anna, who's come without her bloke.'

'Been with him long?' Clive asked, swinging Anna into the dancing.

'Some weeks.'

'And ditched him already?'

'He's Japanese. And he wouldn't like this kind of party.'

'Oh dear, oh *dear*, how kinky!'

Anna escaped Clive as soon as she could. She was drinking more than she should, looking from person to person, moodily watching. Who were these people? They seemed a different species. She was disappointed. This was supposed to be a

68

beginning but she couldn't, although she smiled and laughed, no she couldn't get rid of this feeling of being an outsider. To questions she replied with: I'm Anna. No talk of widowhood, no talk of children (no one wants to be reminded of them), no talk certainly of Japanese. It was a test to see if she had enough skin-deep to interest another person; and it seemed as if she wasn't going to pass. The chatter and babble swirled round her, so why should she be thinking of the fox, and following that the strange figures of the fox women that Hideo had shown her? She still did not know what she was supposed to understand. What was clear was that she had nothing to bring to the party, nothing dazzling like the stories she'd been listening to of weekends in Cannes, of a new group in Soho, of the money made with some deal; only the grisly tale of a fox, and some unexplained telephone calls.

It was maybe a couple of hours later when Anna quietly slipped down the hall and moved through it onto the front path. The smell of fresh green at her feet filtered through the thick smoke that came out with her.

Of a sudden she was seized from behind, and swung firmly round.

'Anna. You're not going!'

'Just popping home to check up, Dave.'

No, no, he murmured, you're not to go, as if he knew she was lying. Had there been someone with him? When he kissed her she complied from curiosity, to see what it was like again. How quickly one forgot. And then one thought, ah yes, that is what it is: the sweetness that is more to do with youth and good health than we'd like to believe. An ill man does not want to kiss; his skin flinches from touch. As if this retreat of Gregory's had been contagious, Anna had become like this too; now gratefully, if only for a moment, she allowed the caress, if not the person . . .

'*Slut*! You greedy whore!'

Anna roughly let go, Dave turned on his wife and slapped her across the face. Janet had hair falling over her eyes, and taking unsteady steps from side to side she jabbed with her fingers at Anna, accusing, slurring her words. 'I only ever see men. Men, aren't you mad for them! It's disgusting. But you're not having any more of him, not any more, too much, too much,' dragging at Dave. Anna could not follow; even hearing them shouting at each other she couldn't understand, and trying to get away found herself pulled back by Janet, strong in her anger, and weeping in loud sobs.

Protesting, herself angry now, Anna shook her off.

'I know he comes over all hours, but we're not . . . tell her Dave, that we're not − '

'Hours he's with you. Hours. And all night!'

'Don't be a fool, Janet.'

Dave had pulled the front door closed behind him, but the windows were open and sounds of jollity, the pulse of music and dance made even this caution unnecessary.

'All night! You know you were out all night, you bastard, David. When that Jap got drunk, you two had it off then. It's revolting.'

'Janet, he came home with me but he didn't stay. Tell her,' she pleaded.

Dave leaning against his door said nothing, he wiped the top of his lip. Anna could feel Janet quivering still where she'd again caught her arm, but her attention was leaving her, and focusing on him; her voice soft with menace: 'So. You've been cheating all round.' They ignored Anna now, intent on each other.

She stepped out into the road: alone. How good to feel warm air. The trees were stirring gently and a waft of scent from blossom came to her. The noises from the party echoed round the houses, yet going up towards her house she had the impression of a scuttling on the path beyond the deep shadow from the yew tree. Had the fox returned? Was it there even now, crouching and watchful in the thick plants? It could cause no further damage. She was putting the key into the lock when in spite of the noise from over the road she heard a squeak behind her – as of the sole of a rubber shoe when it's turned on the ball of the foot. Her body broke out into a sweat. Had Dave followed? But the shadows did not turn into a man. Someone there?

The moon made such deep shadows. At the side of the yew the darkness appeared more solid somehow; as she concentrated on it, it appeared to move. Unnerved, she needed to know if Hideo was in the house.

He was sleeping on his back, his face in sleep smooth and untroubled, an interloper in her own house. His eyes when shut tipped at the corners. Still uneasy in her own room she looked out again at her night-transformed garden. That sensation of being watched was only by night creatures; and she'd already suffered enough damage from them.

The bell cut into her sleep so that she didn't know how to act, feeling the dream of the fox slipping away while her anxiety took on a new cause. Eyes weighted with sleep she tried to focus on the clock. Groaned. She'd come back very late and some small personal alarms were beginning to go off. The ringing was persistent.

'Mrs Dean.'

'Oh no. Do you know what time it is in England?'

'It's you we want to speak to, Mrs Dean.'

Anna waited angrily. Her head swam: too much drink, too little sleep.

'We would like to ask some questions.' The silken voice was cool and light. Anna, wide awake now, realized what was disturbing: the words were all correct, but monotonous, they had no emotional colour, they lacked any tone. It was the English of someone who has learnt too perfectly by the book.

And for some reason there were more pronounced echoes on the line.

'Please will you be so obliging to tell us if Mr Ishida is well, now?'

'Perfectly. It was only a cold.'

'Will you please wait?' There was silence.

Anna shifted her feet. There was a pain between her shoulder blades.

'Mrs Dean?' (The operator, she supposed, had to listen to the questions, and then translate.) 'Did Mr Ishida have many expectorations?' This was said with great precision.

'Not many.'

'Will you repeat that, please?'

'Not very much.'

Again there was silence. Anna could imagine the answers going round the world, being translated, and the subsequent questions being translated back for her. Totally ridiculous.

'What did he eat while he was ill, can you tell us, please?'

'Nothing much. Just a bit.'

'Can you tell us exactly what he ate?'

'Some soup,' she shouted.

'He ate some soup and also perhaps some rice can you tell us, please?'

'I don't remember the rice.' Ah, Anna was thinking, some coffee, hot, and black with sugar, that would do the trick for me.

'Will you be so kind to wait a moment, please?'

Anna propped herself against the wall. Her eyes shut, and her elbow must have brushed against the telephone rest, for she heard it being disconnected. She sighed and went downstairs but while she was making the coffee the phone rang yet again. She let it ring until the coffee was ready and put herself on a chair, with an irritated resignation lifted the instrument.

'Mrs Dean? Please can you tell us if Mr Ishida has had regular bowel movements after his illness?'

Anna passed her hands over her eyes as if this would help her to hear, then took some coffee. 'Who am I talking to?'

'Mrs Dean can you please tell us – '

'Can you tell me *who* I am talking to?'

In this quick interchange the voices had overlapped. The echoes of women's voices, the absurdity of it, this little conspiracy of caring.

'Hello,' Anna called, '*who* am I talking to?'

'This is Tokyo. Are you there?'

Losing her temper made her pompous. In England it's considered bad taste to . . . But the real absurdity of what she was about to say caught the words in her throat. She put down the phone. She was going back to bed.

Nick sprang through the kitchen door. 'Oh good, you're up. I want my breakfast. I was awake ages before the telephone.'

'It's only half-past seven, it's Sunday, I'm going back to bed, I feel awful.'

He had already clambered up to get cereal; his bare toes curled for balance round the bar of the stool. 'You can't be feeling terrible. You're laughing.'

'As you get older, Nick, you'll find you can do both at the same time.'

Fay passed her on the stairs. Who was it?

Japan.

'Oh them again.'

Over the banisters Anna called, 'Them?'

Fay called up, 'They rang for Hideo last night.'

Anna got back into bed. She pulled the sheets over her head which was aching. She heard Hideo go into the bathroom. She heard him clearing out his lungs. She buried her head in the pillow. She was beginning to remember last night.

*

'You're looking pale, Anna.'

'Hangover.'

'Oh good,' said Anna's mother.

You're not going on the barge holiday, they said, more's the pity. Heaven-sent opportunity and so good for the children . . .

'And how's your lodger?' her father asked. 'Don't know whether it's just because of you but I do seem to see many more around than I used. In London at least. Of course they're moving their industry here for one thing – expect they're glad to get out. So little space for living there, they tell me.'

'Yes, but it's their year, isn't it,' Anna's mother was saying, her manner, bright and encouraging, there was the Exhibition on, and the BBC running all those films, not that they'd seen any what with the garden to do . . . Her mother had been determined to be positive since Anna had been bereaved. Life had to go on, and there were the children to think of.

But they were more concerned when they heard about the telephone calls.

'Oh it must be his mother,' Anna's mother said with a little laugh, 'for no one younger could afford the expense, could they? Even so, I'm sure I've never worried so about you children when you were away. Does he ever say anything?'

'Only once when he refused to answer.'

Her father was of the opinion: quite right too. When a young man's away, he's away and should be left alone to get on with his own living. That was one trouble with modern communications. And of course if he was ill one could understand . . .

'Or in some kind of danger, but here, particularly here, where could he be safer?' Anna's mother laughed heartily at the thought of murder and mayhem in a London suburb.

'And anyway,' added Anna crossly, 'it is nothing to do with me.'

Of course not.

'Professor Otaki made a point that they'd chosen England rather than America, and when you come to think of it the family must be influential.'

Other benefits had occurred to Anna's mother: perhaps she would get asked back to Japan? And wouldn't she like to go there, those exquisite temples, and they say the countryside is ravishing?

'Well I don't know . . . ' Anna's father had a way of stroking his chin, feeling for stubble with the tips of his fingers while he thought a thing through: it was a nervous habit he'd brought back since he'd been a prisoner of war. 'I used to think I had some idea of the German mentality, but the Japanese? I know very little about them, and yet they are a force to be reckoned with, nowadays. They have so much money. Want to be top dog. Though what that's got to do with your young man – '

'He's not her young man,' Anna's mother said too quickly, then blushed. Both parents became quiet. Anna sighed to herself. She knew they wanted her to marry again; to find a father for the children, to become ordinary and respectable and restore herself to society somehow. She would not mention the newspaper cuttings, nor the visitors to the house. That would only add to the mystery, without clarifying a thing.

And really, she insisted, there was no need for them to come over every single weekend, not any more. It was a relief to them. 'And anyway, love, we are just at the end of the telephone, which is such a comfort.'

*

75

On a weekday, Anna walking in the park found it newly green, and after the rain the ground shone with an almost greasy sheen. If one went steadily it was possible to make the circuit in three-quarters of an hour. Going to the party had opened her eyes. Or was she at last catching up with the rest of the world? Where had this fierce materialism come from? Had it always been there, and had she been in some way protected from it through being a young mother? It had not occurred to her before that this state might be a protection as well as being protective in its own right. And she hadn't liked the people at the party. She'd found out that the marriage of Dave and Janet was merely a convenience; she'd also since found out that David who'd always (so he said) had a partiality for her, had used that as a shield behind which to carry out other manoeuvres of an amorous sort. He had made her his alibi, damn him. She felt a fool. A little pathetic creature expecting sympathy while the world cavorted. So, she could rely on them no longer; and felt again bereaved for she'd thought of them as accessible friends, whose faults one forgot.

Midway was an oak on a rise of ground which had been struck by lightning; half the trunk was split, and blackened by fire. In spite of this and the hard winter, the other half of the tree was pushing out small yellow-green leaves. Rabbits lived at the roots. Leaning against this tree and letting the watery sun hit her face, Anna tallied her friends onto her one hand. A woman with children at home is one of the busiest and one of the most lonely of creatures. No longer interesting as a woman, used up, automatically deemed boring. There were people around her, yes; but hardly any she could count on. Why had it happened? She did not think she was especially unlikeable. It was because she had let things lapse. For good reasons. But only now did she begin to realize what it all implied. It would take time to change things.

God knows what they got up to in that crowd but she didn't want any of them as acquaintances except for a nice woman called Clare. A flush came into her face at the thought of how she'd been nearly trapped by her dependence on Dave. It would be some time before she'd rid herself of the accusations which had caused so much laughter to those party-goers who'd come out to hear the fun. One good thing, Hideo was hardly likely to know anything of what had been shouted up and down the road. She'd manage without these persons. Yet still the words stung: can't talk about anything but her beautiful Japanese. And the talk which she hadn't known of massage parlours, the Japanese way of sex, the sadism. It made one wince.

Hideo was sitting with his legs tucked neatly, hands resting on his knees. A smile of some beautitude passed over his face when she walked in, then he ignored her. The questions she needed to ask stuck in her throat: he was an adult, why was he behaving like a child? His smooth face was a mask. And a mask, she was thinking, and the donning of a mask suggests a strong desire to conceal and mystify. But she was learning fast; the politeness and the elaborate forms are there to force conformity and to avoid that pit of hell: the confrontation.

Prominent on the hall table she saw the parcel. Addressed to the family, so she opened it. It was prettily packaged and she went with it in her hand, smiling and disarmed, to show it to Hideo.

'Thank you. They're from you?'

'Sorry?'

'These sweets. Are they from you?'

'Oh,' he said leaning over as she held them out, 'the man brought to door.'

'Yes. But did you send them?'

'They are Japanese sweets. Very good.'

'Yes. I know. But do you give them to us?'

'I. No. I did not send.'

The parcel came from a shop in central London. Could it be from his mother?

'I think not.' He was definite.

In the evening the children gloated over the sweets but Anna would not let them have any. Nick sulked as one would expect. 'How can it be a mistake? You're horrible!'

But she had to ring the shop and ask who ordered them. Perhaps it had been Professor Otaki here on business, she suggested brightly, though she doubted it. But in the morning Anna knew she'd been right for the post brought another letter from the City, again including a newspaper cutting. A girl answering from the shop, speaking in that light tone Anna had grown accustomed to, said the purchaser had been a man and perhaps a Japanese gentleman, so sorry, but no more information.

'So, Michael, what do you think, please?'

Sitting with her over a drink, wrinkling his face into an expression of distaste: the colours alone would put him off.

'You don't take it seriously?'

'Has someone got it in for you round here? Been up to anything?'

Anna blushed.

'Aha! Well, I didn't send them. Nor this cutting. It looks like a woman's trick to me. I mean, what a silly thing, after all.'

'Suppose I'd given them to the children.'

'Rather them than me. Too lurid for my taste.'

'But they *might* be poisoned!'

Michael was silenced by this. They read the cutting carefully. It told of a gang in Osaka demanding millions of yen and threatening to poison all sweets on sale through the city. Two people had already died. All stocks had been taken away.

It was baffling. The cutting from an English newspaper.

'Well . . .' Michael's coolness that she'd remarked before had grown. He was a conventional man and he did not like things out of the ordinary, and now that he thought she'd made an enemy, this made him, predictably, suspicious of her. This much, however unfair, was obvious. But he was a kind man and promised to keep in touch, struck when he stopped at the door by Anna's worried look. It was a horrid thing to happen, but surely a one-off thing. Best put it behind her.

Anna said to herself she'd keep quiet. There was nothing to go to the police about. Of course not, and they had far more serious things . . . But she'd be on her guard. As she passed the mirror in the hallway she caught a sight of herself moving, and in thinking of Michael also thought of Louise: 'Things happen to you Anna, strange things.'

With the coming of the warmer weather, the gardens blooming, people in lighter clothes were correspondingly lighter-hearted, more actively social. Anna found herself more aware of these social patterns than she had been in the past, observing from somewhere further away as one would observe the flight of birds or the foraging of ants. And as she herself got caught up in it – there was so much going on in the town and at the schools, where it was continually assumed that she had all the time in the world to give – the result was day following day in a kind of extended domestic round, this time involving the parish and out into London itself.

She had rather blackmailed Michael, wanting to talk over with someone detached her feeling that Janet might be behind the newspaper cuttings. She'd accused Anna, she'd been hysterical, so perhaps . . .

The restaurant where she met Michael was chic, and the company interestingly suave and, thank heaven, young. But Michael marred the pleasure by talking non-stop about his daughter and Louise. Listening, Anna began to feel used (wryly conceding it served her right): used by Louise who had thrown them together almost certainly with intent, and used also by Michael who had his own reasons beyond philanthropy for coming to see Anna. She had been part of their duel. Anna, still listening, also found she didn't understand herself either but that somewhere, something had been quietly repairing and that she now suddenly knew she was nearly ready, wanting to love again, to have a man again. She knew just as well that people would not easily let this happen; whatever they said about it, the widow was viewed with more suspicion than charity. Such women are dangerous. Both Janet and David had seen her through the haze of their own inclinations. She sighed. Michael was not the right man. She could not, any more than with Gregory, get near him.

'Really, what it comes to is that I can't get over Louise. Sorry, Anna, what a bastard to bring you to lunch to hear this.'

Was Michael thinking she was in love with him, that this was why she'd been encouraging?

'You're such a comfort. For you know what loss is.' Michael was dejected, and perhaps had not taken into account the different levels of loss. Oh dear, Anna was thinking, this is how it is: one can feel sorry, but at the same time you can see how the woeful countenance makes people want to run. As they would run from her? Was this why even when there were offers of help she still felt alone?

'But it is better surely to be able to feel deeply,' she said playing with the inevitable red rose in its silver vase.

'Better to have loved and lost you mean.'

Oh dear. 'Yes,' she said stoutly. 'It's a cliché but true.'

He called for the bill. 'I'd like us to go on being friends. It's

80

of more value than lovers' friendship.' He took her hands warmly. Tension eased, he appeared younger; they might well stay friends.

When she reached home she found Hideo sitting on the floor in the front room, his face having a closed but contented look. She found this cheering.

'Well, that's the end of Michael.' What made her say that?

Hideo sucked in his breath. He bowed slightly over his bent knees. How supple he was. 'Ah, *so* . . . *desu.*'

Ah so, Anna said in agreement.

The telephone had that quality she recognized immediately now. But the voice was male. The accent was not good; one could feel the concentration behind it, the deliberate placing of words. It was a voice used to command, hoarse and rather breathless, but Anna was stronger than she had been two months ago and when there was no reply to her query of where the call was coming from, she put the receiver down. It rang again after a short interval, and the man straightaway said, 'I am ringing from Hong Kong, Mrs Dean, and I want to talk with Ishida Hideo.'

Hong Kong, a man. She watched Hideo as he fitted the earpiece, and saw him stiffen and stand alert as if at attention. *Hai*! like an army recruit at parade. She was already moving away when she was rocked on her feet by hearing him speak English. It was a passable English and more fluent than she'd ever heard. In indignation she swivelled towards him. He was flushed. Mounting in a huff to her room, she lifted the telephone there. Hideo had stopped talking. The man from Hong Kong in curt words seemed to be issuing some order. No hesitation there, and no questioning.

Soon Hideo came up to his room. He shut himself away, leaving her fuming and frustrated. It was none of her business.

So yes, admitted, it was nothing to do with her. The next day in his room everything was neat. On the table, as well as the writing pad (now filling with seemly phrases) was a tape recorder, small, and expensive. Also an airline timetable, and his passport. Was he leaving? She went cold.

Restlessly she moved around the house. She studied her face in the mirror, trying to see herself as others saw her. It was not much use. Someone somewhere disliked her so much they wanted to disturb her peace. This was the unpleasant fact. One saw people were spiteful, and sometimes vicious, yet try as she might she could not see what the person or persons were trying to say. The links were children, disaster or malice, and Japanese. It had to be someone who knew her. But who could resent her, and why? And if it was a warning . . . of what?

Out in the garden there had been a light shower, and drops of water collected together and then rolled slowly off the tips of the rose petals. The garden gave the appearance of being beautiful, private and enclosed. But it had been invaded; and the invasion of her private world had crept through ways she had been used to think of for comfort and support: through that telephone, the post-box, an invasion along wires, insidious. At the far end of the garden even a slight movement made her start, but it was only the neighbourhood cat nosing through the undergrowth. It was a bushy cat with a proud fox-like tail held erect. It surveyed Anna, then went still. She followed its gaze upwards. The swallows had arrived.

'So you understand a great deal more than you let on.'

Hideo smiled politely.

'The children say you speak well with them.'

And still he didn't talk.

'Is it your mother who rings in the morning?'

He bent his head. *Hai*.

It enraged Anna he should use Japanese.

'She's concerned about you then.'

Still he would not look up. 'Yes, she is concerned.'

'Perhaps she thinks I don't look after you.' She was forcing him to say no. He could not bring himself to say no.

'She does not think that. She knows you are kind.'

Anna did not want to be called kind.

'She doesn't trust me then.'

There was silence.

'And that man who rang,' Anna went on in increasing frustration, 'who was he?' and then saw his hands: he'd made them into fists and bent them inwards to the wrists tightly; there was tension right up into his shoulders, and she was looking at the top of his head. Softer, she asked about whether his father was a businessman and what kind.

'He is businessman.'

Yes, Anna thought: my father is serious and he plays golf and what else does he do? None of her concern. And some demon made her ask, did he play golf?

'Yes, he plays goff.'

She couldn't help a snort of amusement. Then he looked up, the face as unmoved as ever but in the dark eyes (in this light, dark brown) was something that had gone before she could see; anger could it have been, or anguish, or even a momentary annoyance which made him get up and walk into the garden. Anna watched him from the window, angry with herself. She considered Hideo's mother, pictured her, maybe wrongly, as an old-style Japanese woman. She saw her from the side, kneeling, thick black hair held up with combs, her head bent gracefully in an attitude of listening, the hair meeting the pale skin at the back of the neck in a point. And she does ikebana.

83

There was a tree to the side of the garden that had not yet put out many leaves, and the rain had gathered in drops along its length and along the twigs. The sun broke out now from the clouds and lit the drops from the side, making them shimmer and catch the colours of the spectrum.

Hideo became part of this beauty and as he moved she could see the back of his neck, the strong shoulders on the lithe body of a young man. Her knees felt shaky; her body, still weak, still not strong enough, chose this way of coping with emotion as she followed him out into the garden to say she was sorry, to say anything.

'Sorry? It is nothing.'

This rose is called Masquerade. The flowers which had been bent over by the weight of the rain were slowly lifting themselves back upright against the wall.

'Is he going?' asked Fay that evening with that intuition children possess.

'I don't know.'

Daring, she faced him with it, standing four square in front of him on her sturdy little-girl legs.

'I leave? Why should I go? You want me to go? Mrs Dean, you want?'

She was independent. She was an adult woman, therefore would sort out her own problems. She would not, except as a last resort, turn feebly to her parents for advice. It would only add to their unsettled feelings about the way life was going – a phrase used mildly by her mother to cover her unease with the younger generation and its doings. Anna's father found it natural having this response; growing older robbed one of the energy to cope and there was nothing nowadays definite to deal with, unlike the War in his youth where issues were clear cut, and where decisions were forced through by the extreme situation. No, she could not ask them.

How easy it was to be left alone. Reticence about prying into someone's private life, embarrassment at grief, compounded by the very human desire to avoid the contamination of illness, all these isolated the person bit by bit, the person herself colluding through circumstance. She had to be vigilant. Her house still had an atmosphere of claustrophobia, yet outside there was nowhere to go that felt welcoming. She would go out with foreboding, asking what might have got into her home while she had left it vacant. Time and again her mind went back to the fox. It also had entered her home by stealth.

Early summer rain, bringing out the scent of flowering trees, the lilac, and laburnum, and the heavy voluptuous syringa. Each morning was a little darker as the vine on the back wall of the house grew inches in the night and drooped flat leaves like hands over the window. The leading fronds wandered in different directions each day until they found a firm grip and held on. A shoot had even insinuated its way between the window and the sill. It would have to be pruned back. One day at this time a pale green envelope containing a pale green and gold invitation arrived from the college for a summer fête in aid of some charity. The charity was going to do well, judging by the price of admission which Anna decided she couldn't afford, but it turned out she was Hideo's guest anyway. And the children too? How generous.

85

Down the road to the college the horse chestnuts were fully out, making Nick, who was prone to it, sneeze every few steps. Fay had on her summer jeans, skipping ahead and twirling round.

Hideo would meet them there.

Fay asked, sliding her hand inside Anna's palm, why he talked a lot to Anna now. What had happened?

'Oh, I heard him talking English on the telephone.'

'Who to?'

'Maybe his father.'

'But why do that?'

Yes, why, perhaps to show how he was progressing.

'Funny!'

The grass in front of the college like a botanical garden was already full of people, with women in saris and kaftans, wondrous plants, the breeze treating blossom and fabrics alike so that all were united in a gentle swirling movement. Anna felt almost invisible in plain cotton. There would be strawberries; and she left the children to explore the sideshows while she sipped golden wine, listening in to that hum of rather haughty English that foreigners tend to learn, and seeing how exotic it must appear to Hideo as it would to her if she were attending a similar event in Kyoto. Stepping backwards to avoid a group already posing for photographs, Anna found herself between three apparent clerics, one British and the other two Middle Eastern. With so many costumes and a programme that stated there were prizes to be awarded for the most interesting get-up, how could one judge the honesty of dog-collars?

With a modest laugh, slightly accented, the British cleric admitted he didn't know why he'd been invited. The two Middle Eastern gentlemen inclined politely: they knew why they had been asked.

'I'm a landlady.' Anna said.

Ah, landlady. Ah.

'Do you have your protegé here?' the man asked her, and on

Anna and the other two looking blank explained it had several meanings of which the most important were: a dependant, or a special sort of friend. 'It's someone who is under the protection of someone else.'

Anna supposed that before she'd arrived they'd been talking linguistics together, but given Hideo's personality the word seemed apt.

'Have you been here long?'

'I've only just arrived.'

'So have we. We were saying we knew no one here. But what a magnificent gathering! Truly international! England,' he explained smoothly as if he had done so times before, 'has always been a melting pot for the races . . . ' Moving away Anna could hear words floating after her ' . . . teaches tolerance of one's fellow-man . . . genuine United Nations . . . '

The Bursar was in the library where Anna went to view an exhibition of students' work, together with some neighbours she knew by sight, who expressed their satisfaction at seeing her there, and their satisfaction with the weather. Perhaps with time her contagious quality was going.

'I do hope', the Bursar said sotto voce, 'that you're not having too many difficulties. If I could only tell you . . . a real nightmare.'

And someone else claimed her attention.

Eating chicken with the neighbours and an over-polite Indian couple, out of the corner of her eyes she could see her children darting around and decided to ignore them, to forget they were there. She was wishing for something to happen. Groups were to give their nationality pageant. 'That promises to be dire.' One could not tell whether the costumes were worn every day or not. Yes indeed, insisted the Indian couple.

Several geishas had taken a pose in front of a cedar of lebanon planted at about the time their country had been first invaded in the last century. Isolated like that they belonged to it, then one of them produced a tiny camera from her sleeve and broke the nostalgic picture. Hideo was not with them. Were they students here too? She saw him at last in a group of young men, encircled so that she hesitated to go up to them, and as she moved tentatively forward she saw that the wine, as before, had gone to his head. In fact, they made an annoying group, attracting some attention to themselves by their boisterous behaviour.

'Lack an enzyme for synthesizing alchohol,' came a voice behind her. 'Funny business, isn't it? Make complete idiots of themselves and proud of it. Get maudlin after, though. I've suffered going around with them in Osaka. Safety valve, given their repressive society.'

Anna turned round, wanting to identify the speaker, but he was already moving away. She'd dearly have liked to talk with him. The geishas, the young Japanese men, and a collection of fluttering Indians were being gently hustled once more towards the tree by what appeared to be a television crew. As they moved ahead of the visitors the cameras started to roll, and Anna saw Hideo suddenly freeze, with a great effort pull himself sober; backing through the people there, he went at a run towards the rear of the grounds and got lost in the shadow of the trees.

Then all groups were caught as in a gust of wind, some being propelled towards the camera, while others were pushed from them, and Anna, now searching for her children, was much taken with the increasingly haphazard movement of people, some swaying towards each other with shouts of laughter, others standing stiffly holding half-full glasses. She went towards the Japanese group in case Hideo had returned or the children looked for her there. She asked a girl if she knew Hideo; the girl giggled, pointing towards a geisha in full costume who tittuped forward and, fan in front of face, squeaked at Anna in a high voice, suddenly dropping the pitch to a man's. Anna saw she was being mocked. Laughter surrounded her. Great joke.

It was the ambivalence of this group that made her uneasy;

she had mistaken one or two of the men for kimonoed women, and at the back she caught a glimpse of one, a pretty boy with eyes still lined with black, and the remains of red staining his mouth.

The arrival of the film crew had made people behave with exaggeration, even the visitors had deepened and widened their gestures for the camera's generous eye. No longer interested, Anna went inside and asked a bored trio of Arabs lolling near the food; they peered through the windows at the crowd outside and subsided into chairs. They were not going to perform. And a woman in her own country asking after her children was of no interest at all.

It was an odd building to be in: long, in places several floors high, it stood on a rise overlooking its lawns. It must have been a private house – the sort with many invisible servants – upon which generation after generation had felt compelled to add extra wings, attics, turrets, a conservatory and out-houses. These in their turn had been added to, improved and reconverted to suit the needs of an international college. More an irritating jumble than a romantic maze, it took Anna some time going round corners and meeting with unexplained doors or dead-ends before she decided that it was not really in the nature of her children to penetrate so far into a strange building. More likely that they were near some food, or playing amongst trees and bushes. It was not unpleasant to wander; there were some study rooms panelled and still with stained glass where the afternoon sun shone through spilling out the colours onto an old tiled floor. And the rooms had been deserted for the outside.

For a time she enjoyed herself, pleased to have an alibi if enquiry was made, but no one asked her business. Tiring, she began to be more determined about where she looked; after more pointless search, during which she uncovered two men in an embrace and found the billiards room, she decided she was being stupid and that the children, after this delay had, of course, gone back home. She'd been too curious. But contented enough she went home through the gentle late afternoon sunshine. The sun warmed her skin, chilled from walking in the tiled corridors. She'd had a good day. And felt again that sense of repair as if in some odd way she'd rejoined the ordinary human world.

The children were not at home. Nor was Hideo.

Could they have gone to the park?

Tea was made, the liquid in the pot even in the sun grew tepid, as she sat there holding onto it, her hands round its sides.

As early evening mingled into supper time she returned to the college. The cedar threw long and heavy shadows over the grass and up the steps of the building. One or two couples were still sitting there. Inside, the cleaning was nearly done; a caretaker shoving the last paper plates into a sack didn't know. One student working in the library. No one in the office.

At the main gate some people lingering. Lost anything?

My children.

Huh, typical. Little terrors.

The lightness of the remark lasted her until she got back into the house. She had been among other parents receiving the pep talk from the police: never let a child go missing longer than two hours, always report. But she didn't know how long their being missing was.

Anna made the decision to go to the park. David and Janet were not in to be asked, nor Dorothy. She asked yet another neighbour to watch out for them; she'd leave (after some moments of doubt) the house open. From the tree where they first learnt to climb, to the pond famous for tadpoles (but not for frogs), to the earth-bare slope where one could slide, further still to the woods where Fay had seen a kestrel nesting, the familiar places made menacing, or even, what was worse, grown non-committal as if to demonstrate how she'd dressed it up with her own images, which she now had to take back. The land did not care about the children, the

90

kestrel, which she saw hovering above her, was oblivious. She hurried back. The house was still empty.

It was a shepherd's delight of a sky. Anger mixed with her exhaustion. Gregory had always insisted she shouldn't mother the children but bring them up to look after themselves. Teach them early that fire burns. But had she told them that people are untrustworthy? She had not wanted them to become suspicious, to be wary before the outer world closed in, any more indeed than a Japanese mother.

Long strands of red were stretching along the sky as the sun set. At the police station Anna tried to make her voice sound reasonable while she described the children. The duty officer took it seriously, of course; this kind of thing, though, happened often as the evenings got lighter; they'd put out a call, please ring back when the children returned, meanwhile as she'd no one else at home, better stay within call as it were . . .

With the window open she weeded in the growing gloom of the front garden. Soon it was easier to see into the front rooms of the houses as their lights came on than to pick out the false from the true in the plants at her feet. As she bent over the dark soil, sensations familiar from caring for Gregory on those last days, of being sick with fear, heavy with it as if legs were stuck with glue to the ground, her fingers now slipping on the trowel, to these were added a despair as heat deserted her body. She had a cold apprehension that something horrible was happening, or could have happened, she couldn't say which. Frantically she looked around; she'd never once thought of being made alone like this. She'd seen the situation as one with them by her, of herself engaged in physical action. How could one fight with nothing? All she could find to fight was her own fear. Which was intensifying as second stretched after second.

Now night. The bats hunting. Images of what could be happening to her young assailed her mind. The thought that life might again take life from her was a torment. She stood rigid under the yew tree. The moment of birth, the moment of love and the moment of death like this: not measurable by clock time. And so she waited, losing hope.

Yet when the phone rang its tinny ring cut through the open window. Anna jumped as if hit. The police?

It was from an outside phone box. The voice was unknown. The intonation she recognized. 'Your children are on their way back.'

She could not reply. The phone went dead immediately. What had she done to be punished like this? She was stifled and sick, and went out to stand in the road.

As she made out the children's shapes, slow and dragging their feet, she felt as if her bowels were dropping to the ground.

In silence she led them in, the lightness of the small shoulder blades under her forearms. Get them to talk about it at once, the duty officer had said.

Sorry, they said. Sorry, sorry.

'We went all the way to Reading and back at a hundred miles an hour! It was a Mercedes,' said Nick. He was still impressed. He hurriedly followed with, 'They said let's see how far we can go there and back before your mother finds out.'

'I wanted to get out but they went so fast,' Fay wept. 'I knew it was wrong but they'd said . . . and Hideo said . . . Anyway, Nick was sick on their car and I'm glad.'

'It was the strawberries.' His face was smudged with black where he was rubbing away his tears. 'And anyway Hideo said he felt bad. He got lost.'

Fay muttered that he was drunk.

Anna was still rigid from suppressed anger. She'd tried brandy but it had in no way helped.

'What have I always, always told you?'

Yes we know, they wailed, they were both shaking, but she felt no pity. They were safe in the house with her. That, for the moment, was good enough.

'Then *why?*'

'They were *friends.*'

'Nick had wine.'

'So did you.'

'What *else?*'

'We sat in the back. I was frightened.'

Their pale shocked faces were pearled with sweat.

Anna had to ring the police back with her lame excuses. They couldn't wait to get her off the line. 'It's tricky, this one. You sleep on it.' But she could not. She lay in wait for Hideo, aching and tossing to and fro. But he did not return that night.

It had been bad behaviour all round that weekend. With the wail of police sirens down on the main road. Around the corner at the greengrocer's, there was talk of the new young foreigners with their huge cars and flashy ways; grumbles about bad parking, impertinence, bad debts. The old man in front of Anna couldn't get past between the wall and this damn great car, and had to walk in the road, what a farce. And Betty, who always gave Anna slightly overweight, said with her Welsh lilt that young people nowadays were all the same, plain silly. But didn't really mean any harm, mind you. Yet when the others had left the shop she suddenly offered the news that she might be leaving. Place isn't the same any more. Fed up with it.

Nothing could appease Anna's anger that day. And she needed no analysis to explain why during the broken sleep she dreamt of her children shrunk to kitten size, trapped in the jaws of foxes. No analysis, even though on the edge of the dream were her hands waiting to sink into the animal fur.

The remembered dream, and her present state of mind were equally clear and hard-edged, so that she knew as she entered the house and sensed his presence that nothing could stop the cut of what she had to say.

'We have to talk. And now.'

Hideo was sitting still and formally. He was dressed in a dark suit as if for an interview or as if he was going on a journey, but nothing could distract her. 'I am very angry. You and your friends took my children away. It was an evil thing to do. Did you know what you had done, or were you too drunk?'

He bowed over his knees. 'I apologize for this.'

His stillness enraged her. The control, the lack of reaction. So it always was, it seemed to her, that one quality one saw in everything they did of an aloof isolation; taking out of the complexity, the untidiness of ordinary living, one thing, the flower, the tree, the rock, the situation, the emotion, ignoring the rest. In all the images she'd seen this was what stuck out.

'It was a dreadful thing to do.'

'I am sorry. *Hazukashii to omii masu* . . . '

'I was so scared I went to the Police, and they said – '

'You spoke to police?' his voice clipped, rapped out.

'Of course. My children were missing.'

'That's not good.'

In justification. 'I did not know where they were in the whole of this city! I had to do something.' Anger again gripped her. 'I thought someone had got them – don't you understand?'

But his face had a shut-up look as if he was taking nothing in. Tears were running down her face, and she reached out, aware that she should not do so, and took him by the shoulders to shake some response, any response from him, and under her hands felt the rapid stiffening and twist of his back, and then the arm coming up to fend her off, clipping instead across her face. She bent over her knees, fumbling for a handkerchief.

94

'We have fun,' he was saying, 'we give them fun, all going together. In nice party. Poor children. Too much sadness! We Japanese like to do things all together. You do not know how we feel.'

Anna's nose was bleeding. It had made a circular red stain in the middle of the white handkerchief. She smoothed it out over her knee. I don't understand a thing. Nothing. Her mind was following the curve of the earth to the other side of the world where there was a story being written touching her own; but it came in a book that read from back to front, with messages she could not read.

'I make mistake to come here.'

Hideo had stayed out all night and robbed her of her immediate measure of anger. Really, now she felt more like weeping, and tiredness was muddling her brain. Many things stayed unexplained, the cuttings were unexplained. Hideo was deep in his thoughts. These new friends of his, who were they?

They were just friends. He went around with them.

How had he got to know them then? Anna was suddenly taken with an idea.

Surprised . . . Professor Otaki arranged.

And who else knew he was here with her?

'The people in my mother's house.'

'Your mother's house? And your father as well?'

No. His father had his own house. 'My mother is geisha.'

His mother and father were not then married to each other?

'My father has already a wife.'

'Oh, I see.'

I see. But she did not see; only that the list of people who knew Hideo's business increased all the time. The Japanese are different, the Oriental mind is different: that was always the gist of the programmes she'd seen. And she had resisted assuming this to be true, first, because she'd thought it typical of journalists to write like this, and also because it seemed a matter of common observation that people were very alike basically. They had the same wants, didn't they?

Are you inscrutable? They sat facing each other. Hideo had put himself in the folded legs position, eyes hidden from her, and a frown coming and going. Then he said, 'I will go away. I am sorry.'

'But where will you go?'

Anywhere. Paris. His voice was dejected.

'But', she insisted, heart beating, 'you were sent to learn English.'

'Yes. My father wants.'

'And your mother?'

'She does not want.'

The screen of cultural difference was between Hideo and herself. She had already forgotten her anger, for her restless brain wouldn't allow her to leave things alone. She had, Englishwoman as she was, to probe, to analyse in the western manner, to search for clues.

The Bursar was coming uneasily down the steps to the college doors as Anna walked grimly up the drive. A light drizzle was falling. She had high heels and a rather tight skirt; Anna waited for her to reach the safety of the gravel. The Bursar, jiggling her car keys, did not look in a sympathetic mood. Couldn't Anna come back some other time? Anna could not, and to make that point said clearly that she wanted to know, indeed had to know more about the Ishida family. The Bursar glanced hurriedly up at the upper windows. One or two of the students who were using the library were peering down from their desks with interest.

Anna followed the Bursar back up the steps. Five minutes only. Reflecting as she did that it is always a mistake for a short woman to wear short clothes. From the back the Bursar had a busy, fussy look which taken with the remark thrown over her shoulder that the students were her chicks confirmed something for Anna. From behind her desk she was even less amiable.

'I know hardly more than you.'

'I think I should know as much as you do.'

'I know so little.'

She was stalling in spite of having to leave for an important appointment.

'The college authorities must be in a position to demand certain bits of information.'

Conceded. But the whole thing. Surely Anna recalled how difficult . . .

The Bursar drummed her fingers on the blotter, passed her hands over her face, and then, correcting the gesture with annoyance, converted it into lighting a cigarette.

'I can't tell you who asked for special concessions to be made. I don't know. It came from top office. I do know it caused headaches. We were already way over numbers and I told them that. One doesn't want to lose the licence, you know.'

'It was from the Principal's Office?'

Grudgingly. 'I don't have to tell you this.' And she looked past Anna to the grounds where the English landscape of old cedar and beech was beginning to steam gently. It was going to be a warm day.

'He was brought over by Professor Otaki. Is that usual?'

'It's not common. They usually come by themselves.'

'Who is Otaki?'

'A professor. I know nothing about him. He wasn't a family friend.'

Persisting. 'And the parents? The mother was always ringing up.'

'She has never once rung me.' (Was this said pettishly?)

'But his father – '

'I have spoken once or twice. But look,' getting up, 'we

shall have to leave it there. Why don't you leave it with me? I'll make enquiries.' Anna saw she was being fobbed off. If she was given names she could make her own enquiries. Tactfully.

'I couldn't do that. Please don't interfere.' The Bursar, standing, intended to go. Anna remained sitting. But if there were these difficulties where could one begin?

There was always something one could do. Standing holding the door open, the Bursar gave a reassuring smile which Anna felt drop on her like the blanket with which one restrains a maddened animal. She passed in front of the Bursar, then stopped, effectively blocking her exit. Mr Ishida is a business-man and rich. Influential, you'd say?

Yes and yes.

She'd come back next week. Down the drive again, tigerish.

Days passed; the warm sun bringing benign tempers, the children watching their behaviour.

'Louise, I have to see you.'

'I want to see you too.'

'No. I mean I need to see you. Someone to talk to.'

There was a slight pause on the telephone before Louise, warm as ever, agreed to a lunchtime in central London. Only a little late she turned heads as she swayed swiftly round tables where Anna waited. She had only it seemed to adjust the muscles in the back of her neck for the waiter to come running. He was the same one who'd appeared to have a limp when Anna had tried to catch his eye.

'Now what is it?' Louise rested her chin on a wrist that had become imperceptibly more elegant; bangles slid further on her arm; her skin was already deeply tanned and Anna wasn't going to ask where and when. Or how. She launched fast into a description of what had been happening. It seemed to take a long time, more than Louise's patience would stretch to for she fidgeted, and ordered after insisting she was paying attention to every word.

'It could have been that Janet. Sort of thing a woman might do. Perhaps she's jealous of him? What's he like? I've always adored that dark man in the samurai films. You know the one. He looks Italian.'

Someone passed who knew Louise. Anna fiddled with food while she waited. The unspoken rule which held that all things female stop the minute a man comes on the scene still held. Years of feminism hadn't eradicated this automatic reaction.

Now then . . . Louise had an air of giving an audience. (What was it about herself that made Anna so sharp in watching the mannerisms of people? Had she become so neurotic that every tic, every facial move was keenly watched and analysed for what might lie behind it?) Louise had stopped eating – though not much effort went into that anyway – to look concerned as Anna built up her picture of awfulness when the children went missing. But a law of diminishing emotions was taking effect. She could feel the old tendency to smooth, to self-mock on each retelling, so that in this reassuring and so English of lunchtimes the story sounded merely an anecdote, not the harrowing experience she had known.

Naughty things, Louise said; what a silly thing to do. 'Really, it was just a prank. Why worry? Put it behind you. Perhaps it's more ordinary there, you know, that sort of larking about. Don't the Japanese love children? And yours are so cute.'

Anna winced.

'Oh I like them. I like children, Anna, it's just I don't want any of my own. What to suggest . . . A holiday? Summer's on its way. Can't you go off somewhere? Ask Michael. Don't look at me like that. Can I help it?' she asked with some satisfaction. 'All right, it was simple of me, but I do like you both and I hoped . . . It will be your saving, Anna. If you had a man around this wouldn't have happened.'

'I have a man around.' Feeling herself redden.

'From what you say he's just a boy. All he wants is to be mothered. Oh heavens,' she said looking over at the door, 'one sees the yellow peril everywhere.'

'They're Chinese.'

'They all look the same to me. And they're always smiling, but where's their sense of humour?' She returned to Anna's affairs and began competently to sort out the bill as she spoke. 'Holiday, Anna. Can I lend you some money? No, better still, let me give you some. I'm particularly flush at the moment.' The radiance surrounding Louise spilt round them both as they moved towards the outside, Anna as the attendant moon finding some of that heat remain with her. A taxi offered itself without asking, Louise merely going the length of Regent Street, 'for companionship's sake', before getting out again, pressing a twenty-pound note into Anna's hand for the fare, saying, 'And you keep the change.' Infuriated, Anna went the rest of the way home by tube. She'd wanted sympathetic advice, not charity.

Standing in the garden which for so long now had been her place for contemplation, listening out for the sounds of children (and it had been impressed on them that they came home with school friends, promptly, and together), she saw that since the drop of petals, fruits were already setting on the cherry tree, and in the garden, without her noticing, the delicate spring flowers were being replaced by the strong thrusting plants of summer. It was still a sort of sanctuary. There were always the uninvited: some to welcome like the swifts already hunting above her, and others . . . With a little twist she lifted a snail from the underneath of an iris. It had already spoilt one bloom, and as she straightened she realized Hideo was looking at her from his bedroom window. How long had he been there? He raised his hand in a sort of salute.

In her fingers the snail had put out its sticky body. One never knew what to do with snails. The fine horns were waving in the space, trying to get bearings; the fleshy fringe of its body touched her finger, and in disgust she hurled it from her and heard it crack. Ashamed, from above she heard the loud laughter.

She had begun to take a daily newspaper again. Damn the expense. Only gradually had it occurred to her that she had cloaked herself in bereavement, hiding while others had made decisions in her name. In all justice she had to work better for the living than she had managed to do for the dead. She must inform herself. It was indeed true there was more discussion and articles about the other side of the world. The impulse behind the exhibitions and films and general talk must have proceeded from some drive begun years before when things Asiatic were something of a joke. She had a compelling reason to find out more, keenly aware of signs of the shrinking of the globe. And she couldn't shake from her mind the consciousness of some drama being played out on the other side of the world, as an illness does in the body of someone else, literally while she slept.

Everywhere felt odd, and carried a faint smell of menace.

Hideo was avoiding her. He would take his breakfast when she left with the children, and be gone when she returned. He stayed out every evening. And Anna no longer had enough to do, was marking time, braced for more trouble. A thin rain came to drench the earth. After a few days everywhere hung in a dripping green gloom as trees grew dense and thick with deep wet shadows under their branches. When the rain stopped and the sun crept from the heavy clouds, a mist came off the ground, carrying with it that mixture of vegetation and dog urine which marked for Anna the end of the sweet scents of new growth, and the beginning of the smell of corruption that was the sign of a hot summer.

*

101

'Yes. Quite on the spur of the moment. And then we thought, why not leave Anna the car?' Her father speaking to her, but looking at her mother. 'I thought another honeymoon might do your mother some good. It's been a hard winter. Nothing but illness and bother. If we go now we're at home for the rest of the school holidays . . . '

'Besides, it was such a bargain,' – her mother tilted her head, smiled her kind smile – 'and we thought that instead of leaving the car at the airport we'd leave it with you. You can take the children out, and perhaps your – '

'You know what she still calls him? "Anna's paying guest." What a snob your dear mother is.'

'Oh Jack!' She gave him a playful dig in the ribs. They were happy to be going away with each other. They'd always been like this. Fondly Anna looked on, pushing out the envious comparison. There was no answer as to why with such an upbringing she hadn't managed a happy marriage herself.

'Well then, will your young man look after you a bit?'

'Mummy, he's not my young man.'

'Your lodger, dear, don't get so tetchy.'

Nick was hopping in and out of the gutter. From the corner of her eye Anna could see her father restraining himself with difficulty. Fay was primly waiting for that inevitable moment when the nerve would crack and Nick would get reprimanded for being stupid.

'Have we been through everything?' With deliberation her father fixed his eyes on the car. 'It's serviced. It's insured. You're insured. We're insured. Anything else, Anna? Anything to tell us. Any problems?'

102

No. Standing there, greeting the neighbours, agreeing to drive them to the airport the following weekend, there was nothing else to say. Anxieties of a vague and unspecified kind can't be taken away in a sponge-bag. They were only away for a month.

'Your Japanese? We still haven't met. Where does he hide?'

'He's a bit shy.' Anna was annoyed. She'd asked Hideo to eat with them, he'd agreed and that was the last she'd seen of him.

'Is he shy, Fay?'

Fay, who had got to the stage of stripping leaves from the privet, said Hideo never stopped talking. This made Nick change his tactics to tell her that was a lie. What with one banal thing and another, the moment passed in which Anna could possibly have discussed anything with her father.

Always outside events took Anna over, and more and more she resented having so little say in her own life. But suddenly asked to do more legal work after a long silence, she didn't want to refuse. This took her past that day when she thought she would revisit the college. Whether it was for this or another reason, the Bursar's secretary conveyed she couldn't see her, that the Bursar would be extraordinarily busy as she was then taking her vacation. Everybody was taking a vacation. Anna, certain she was being fobbed off, was standing fuming at having by this delay provided a perfect excuse, and assessing the chances as she stood in the corridor of being able to storm the office, when someone passing called hallo.

It was a woman Anna's age. We met, yes, at David's house . . .

Prettier than Anna remembered, Clare wrinkled her face at the mention of the Bursar, which made Anna warm to her at once. 'But I've not been here long, and I'm only just finding what a wheeler-dealer place I'm working in. College politics I keep out of, but if there's anything . . . '

Clare's office, built on a mezzanine, overlooked the length of the library through a wall of glass. 'I feel a bit like a jailer here,' she said lowering her voice. 'The students often look up, so I moved my desk to the side.'

Anna looked down into the library. At the far end a foot stuck out with a telltale sock. 'Do you know the students?'

'Most of them to talk to. All by sight.'

They talked over coffee until Hideo emerged from his alcove for a book. Anna sunk back, but he didn't look up. 'What about him?'

'Hideo Ishida? He's very charming, that one. Most of the Japanese are pleasant, but they're hard to get to know. It's surface politeness, one feels. But he's rather different.'

'Why is he different?'

'Well, it's funny you should pick him out. Everybody gets tense about him. I can't think why, unless he's got something wrong with him I haven't been told about . . .

'Ah I see,' after having it explained to her. 'That's why you're here? I don't think you need to worry about him. The Bursar looks after him especially well.'

It was not the full story; Anna tried to recall if Clare had been told anything about her, and almost at the same time decided it was irrelevant. She had to stop calling on the dubious support a widow might command.

He put in many hours down there in the evening. But she knew that.

No, Anna said. She'd thought he was out with friends. 'He often claims he's out with friends.'

Down the length of the room the students, sitting with their backs to the central aisle, were a random mixture which seemed, nevertheless, balanced at first glance between race and colour. Clare, following Anna's scrutiny of the occupants, asked if she'd met any fellow students.

'Only at the do. Clare – '

'I have to go,' Clare was saying gently, 'but if there's anything . . . ?'

'Could you come round one evening, would your husband mind?'

Amused by this tentative query; Clare, shaking her head, already worked two evenings. 'He won't think anything of it.' And she'd like to, thanks.

But when Clare did come round Anna regretted her impulse. It seemed on this telling to be a vague and unconvincing fiction; somewhere along the way the episode of the fox had inserted itself into the account, provoking a look of disbelief, and as she tried to sort things out stage by logical stage, she still felt the facts evaporate and float away as so much hot air.

There was a silence and then Clare said she didn't understand.

Anna put her hands to her temples.

'What's behind it? It's crazy!'

As the relief fed into her that she was to some extent believed, Anna relaxed.

'But are all these things connected? The telephone calls . . . '

'Those come from the family. At least I assume – '

'But the letters . . . It's the children being driven off that's nasty. Children *do* go missing and are never seen again. Children *are* found molested. Or dead. And that's terrible. Of course you were right, Anna. Why haven't you asked him to leave?' She had a nice open smile, and something about her, fresh and bright, reminded Anna of the clear blue of forget-me-nots in spring.

'Oh no,' she replied, too hastily. Oh no. Her mind slid away from the possibility. He was more real to her now – strange as he continued to be – than her English friends. 'I don't like being bullied, and the things are so absurd that as you say I can hardly believe it's happening. Rather like the fox . . . so strange to have it there. It was so beautiful, odd.'

'Have you thought of writing to the parents?'

They were separated. In any case, no Japanese.

Someone could translate.

Another idea. It was decided to write to Professor Otaki.

Dear Professor Otaki, I hope you are well. Some of your compatriots are trying to scare me . . .   Dear Professor, I am concerned about Hideo's activities, which are not what you would approve . . .   Dear Prof., Some strange and inexplicable events . . .   None of this would do. Eventually, she wrote something, but so much was left unsaid. The feeling of being watched, the eerie sensation of being driven towards a trap.

One evening Clare rang: a young woman not normally on the campus had called for some books. A bright girl, not easily impressed, her father was influential in Japan, and she did say after some persistent questioning that Hideo's father was very influential, and 'known', she'd said.

One could imagine the persistence needed. Well known?

'She said so. And spoke with a certain respect. There's another thing. Things aren't quite right here. Have you noticed the quick turnover of tutors? Well of course, you're

106

just supposed to be his landlady . . . Anyway, the college finances are not that rosy. I found out the horrid way as I may lose my job. Payments haven't been coming in. And there's some scandal brewing about students who've had advances and such.'

'I can see why the Bursar doesn't want to know me,' said Anna. 'Hideo must be a valued customer. I'm sure he pays his bills. They have a great sense of honour about that.'

The place would crumble without the rich foreign students.

'That wouldn't worry me in the least.'

'A lot of people would be out of a job! You know, Anna, the Bursar is a bitch in some ways, but she has to deal tactfully with a hundred rich spoiled kids who haven't left home before. What I've been learning! They go wild, drugs, the lot.' She sighed. 'How things do change. When I think how happy I was in this job. Oh, and listen. Richard and I were in the park very early, and over by the high hill – the one where they slide in winter – were three Buddhist monks all in their yellow robes! So odd! I'm glad you can laugh. Do you think they'll turn up on our doorsteps to convert us? Another thing: come to supper. Bring Hideo too.'

'I'll have to ask Janet to babysit. Dorothy's away.'

'But Janet's been gone weeks. And I don't think Dave's there either.'

Anna went to the window. The curtains opposite were the same. The lights were perhaps on automatic timeswitch. She shrugged. Time passed in such a jumpy way. But she would have sworn someone was still living there.

'She's gone to Cardiff with some man or other.'

'Weeks ago?'

'I think so. Yes. Why? Is it important? Everybody knew it was bound to happen.'

It was nothing. Never mind. In the hall Anna stood by the mirror. She studied her face soberly as if to tell the woman within that she was a fool. Of course dislike of Anna could

107

never have been such an abiding obsession. Janet would have been far too busy about her own affairs.

There were a very few more days before the children broke up for the summer holidays and became a full-time responsibility. And if you tried, as an English woman you could pass the time pleasantly enough if the money was not too tight. One could go on trips, one could amuse. One could stay safely penned in if one chose, but she didn't want this either for them or herself. No ice-cream and currant-bun summer. She visited the cemetery. Already the granite chips on Gregory's grave were growing green mould, and as she stirred them with her hand she found herself talking to the absent father in her mind, of how the children had grown. How things changed in some ways, and not in others.

The very next day they changed again. The telephone woke Anna early. The voice was light, and lilting and polite as before, but it had been such a gap of time that Anna had an indignant desire to protest. As she hesitated, the voice, more insistent than ever before, added, 'We are in a hurry.' Anna knocked hard at Hideo's door. Recently she'd not known whether he was in or out either in the day or night, but her curiosity had caught her.

'Is there trouble at home?'

She had to repeat it. He made a great effort like a man turning a boat in mid-stream, saying words to the effect that it was nothing, then mumbling, 'It is dippicurt,' stopped and got his mouth in the right frame to add, 'My mother is ill.'

'You have to return?'

Emphatically he said no. His father said not. There was no

point in more sleep, so down to breakfast, pulling the newspaper from the letterbox on her way.

The garden half in shadow, half early sun, marked the division with a pearly sheen of dew over the part the sun hadn't touched. The birds undisturbed worked over the grass; already one could hear the shriek of hunting swifts. Too soon always the gentleness of spring overrun by this bold jostle of summer. And yet it was exciting, this energy from summer. There were weeds in her garden.

The disasters of others collated through the night announced themselves in the usual way in thick black letters which, as if to say you can never stay entirely untouched, left a stain on the fingers as she read. Coffee dripped unsteadily through the clogged filter, measuring time in the same way. The news on the overseas page was rarely amusing but today was different. She grinned to herself. The Japanese organize into groups even to commit crime. Particularly to commit crime. And efficiency and allegiance are as valued here as anywhere else. Thousands of gangsters defying the police had turned up at an off-shore island dressed in their best and carrying presents for the swearing-in of the new head of the crime syndicate. How polite! What presents are appropriate? A new gun? A box of bullets gift-wrapped? The new head had been elected in a 'democratic fashion'. Some of the men assembled there (the account went on) had stood up to make an announcement of dissent. One man had thoughtfully provided himself with full press coverage, and invited the television. Like other traders, going international. This was a professional approach. With his best manners he regretted that he could not accept the majority decision for the new boss.

This was the first time she'd heard of Yakuza, and she read soberly of their interest in extortion and prostitution. Drinking coffee which no longer tasted quite so good, she found that what was worrying the police was how they were diversifying into other areas, like hard drugs and laundering money. With the same painstaking attention their country-men showed in business, these gangsters also applied to making vast profits. That apparently inspired respect.

In all seriousness a police spokesman stated that the harmony of the group (so valued, as Anna knew) was broken here with gangsters dividing into factions. They did not know their place. It was not good news. Gang warfare was inevitable.

What a curious quirk, this politeness, like those romantic films about the Mafia where they courteously bid farewell before gunning you down. The piece obsessed her, and she didn't know why: drifting round the house, not getting anything done, fiddling unnecessarily with cushions; even opening a book she'd borrowed about the Japanese mind, but throwing it down in irritation at the stupidity of reading about the motives of a man living in one's own house. For they claim being alike. Near the latter half of the afternoon, thinking of the children her brain jolted into life. She was right. The cutting from the paper attributed the spoiling of the supermarket sweets to the workings of a gang. In England or America this might have been the work of an environment group anxious about poisonous addit-ives. In Japan it was quite clear; it was done to sow fear, and extort money.

Why didn't Hideo eat supper any more? The children complained: it was light now in the evenings, they didn't have homework to do, so why couldn't they go to the park to play? The garden was boring. The road outside was boring. There was nothing to *do*. Nick decided Hideo didn't eat supper because he couldn't stand food messed about. 'I can't either.' He poked at his meat.

'No. He's worried,' Fay said.

'That's stupid. He likes to go out and eat seaweed and raw fish.'

'His mother is ill,' Anna put in. She was concerned about Hideo's obvious depression. The signs of it in his room.

110

Both children looked up, eyes anxious. They nodded in understanding. 'Will he have to go back?'

'He says not.'

Fay demanded why not. He should go back.

Nick didn't want to eat any more. Not even a pudding she'd made for them. 'Is she very ill?' They knew that you have to do everything for people who are ill, and even that is never enough.

'I don't know. Probably not, because otherwise of course he would go.' Fay put down her spoon, appetite gone; she was thinking of her father.

'But I'm all right,' Anna said, 'perfectly all right. Nothing wrong with me.'

There was no more talk of leaving, and being ill.

The sun set in a clear sky. They helped take out some of the less attractive weeds, though from sentiment the dandelions could stay, and Fay blowing their seeds all over the garden for that time when spells begin reached nine o'clock. Sad that this place so lovingly tended nevertheless felt like a pen: a place where wild things could enter, but where they were held in.

This talk of being special. They had a psychic need to be special, and by insisting on difference made it appear true. They approached things from a different angle, of that Anna was convinced, but reached the same goal in the end. It was the news that morning that there were villains in every country that decided her.

And it was at nine, somewhat after nine, and so nearly missed . . . At the end of the television news it was a new idea to add an item amusing, or odd, or offbeat, as a kind of sweet after all the seriousness before, the nasty medicine one was obliged daily to take if one had any interest in the world at all. And there in the sun earlier that day, Anna saw the arrogant saunter of the gang members as they arrived by helicopter and plane and boat at the island where their meeting was to be held. In those dark suits, like businessmen

111

they held their bodies in that stiff way she conjectured as if in revolt from the mental pressure of their mother's hand pushing them into a bow. Though Anna saw at the back of the major group some indeed begin to bow, and bow deeply as if in homage. As the respectful camera homed nearer, the spokesman took a small step forward and with a careful, modulated smile said he regretted he could not accept the decision to elect . . . the voice-over reminding one that it had been a democratic vote and that this was now being contested. Now the man ceased; deliberately turned his back to the camera; and as he did so the man behind him and to one side came into view.

Anna waited up for Hideo. He looked enquiringly. What trouble? She refused to tell him anything and when the late news began restrained herself with difficulty. She saw him jerk up as the same clip came on again. No revolution elsewhere had pushed it out; it could be of minimal interest to an English audience, and she couldn't guess why the piece had been chosen until there was an explanation: this was a sign of the increasing international power of crime syndicates, causing world-wide concern. It was the first time a Yakuza member had so openly appeared on television. But don't ask why.

Again the men with a contemptuous swagger descended from the planes. Again the spokesman regretted, and as he moved Anna laid her hand on Hideo's arm. So did he agree? She watched his face, saw it change, affirming she was right, that the man behind they both knew: that it had been Professor Otaki.

Hideo sat with his hands spread on his knees, tense, his

112

head bent forward. In spite of her fears of the unpredictable she did feel a calm somewhere, and recognized the emotion as that which comes when some apprehension is given shape, and is no longer imaginary. 'So what do you think?'

He sighed. Muttered in Japanese.

'That was Otaki?'

'*Hai*. Yes. I believe so.'

'What does your father do, Hideo?'

His father, he said as if in a lesson, had a business in many things; construction companies, hotels, many things.

'And Otaki works for him?'

He was surprised. 'No,' he said firmly.

'So what does he do?'

Hideo thought and then with some doubt came out with the suggestion that Otaki was something to do with drugs.

'Drugs? Pharmaceuticals, you mean?'

He grimaced at the word. Otaki was important. 'Maybe he is consultant.'

Why then had he come to London with Hideo?

'I do not know. His work perhaps? Maybe.'

Anna had things coming back to her: of how Otaki had stressed that England was 'safe', safer than America. Trying to piece things together in her mind, the pieces still would not fit. She told Hideo what she had done. How she had written to Otaki about the 'letters'.

How many days? He was alarmed.

'Two days ago.'

'It takes a week for letters.'

So what did he think? 'I think there is big trouble here. Not good idea.'

Exasperated, she knew that now, but she had to do something.

Why?

Why? This was no time for practising Zen.

'It is a time for Zen.'

Meditation was not Anna's way of solving problems. But

113

looking at him, she knew she was completely out of her depth. His nationality and poor understanding of words had made difficulty enough, but now events were immeasurably complicated by the standing of his parents.

Hideo began talking of his mother, of how she hadn't wanted him to leave. He'd lived with his mother, or his mother's grandparents until the previous year when his father had adopted him.

'She says she has the one child, and so she does not like it but she accepts. She . . . wept,' – he looked enquiringly at Anna over this word – 'but accepted. Japanese women accept more than you, I think.' She'd had her own house, and her own money already settled on her, but at the same time as the adoption the father had taken another mistress and it had been all finished between them, and Hideo had to go to live with his father. He'd dropped all shyness during this account, and Anna, sagging back to sit comfortably on her heels, could look up into his face, ashamed at her assumption of his slowness. It made her hot to think of it.

A small frown was creasing the fine skin. He said looking at her, 'She is proud woman. Very jealous. She asks all the time about you.'

'About me?'

'Maybe . . . she sent the letters to you.'

'Could she do that?'

He nodded. She could do that. 'She can arrange many things. She is clever.'

Anna's imagination rearranged the picture in her mind. She tried to fit a face to this woman, but failed; she saw her in outline bending to alter and trim the angle of a branch; no longer in kimono, no longer kneeling.

'And your father, who telephoned from Hong Kong. He wanted to test you?'

'He does not talk English well. I have to talk very well.'

'So you can work for him?' He was silent for some time, and she went on, 'What sort of work?'

114

It was nearly midnight. Outside a wind had come up, and through the windows she could see the trees bending back and forth. There was one light only showing across the street. She couldn't get used to how one's life was interfered with in the late twentieth century, indirectly from a remote control, through wires, using electric pulses. 'It's preposterous!'

'What did you say, that word?'

'It's absurd. All of this is very stupid,' and she beat her fists together, and trying to get up found her legs would not move, and she fell over sideways against the couch and weakly began to cry.

'Ha, Anna-San, no.' He sounded frightened. 'Shall I give you massage, Anna-San?' He got down behind her, putting a hand on her shoulder. Ever since she had watched him do origami she had been keenly aware of his fine hands. The way he touched those things is the way he touches a woman. 'My mother says it helps . . . ' It took a lot to make Anna cry these days, but now she had begun it had to have its way and she couldn't stop. But his other hand joining, he began gently but firmly to massage, the thumbs searching out the tight muscles, making them unknot. At what point it ceased to be help and became something other she could not say, but he whispered something and it sounded like a plea. She hadn't moved. Her face still pressed into the cushions, in a state of waiting, afraid to show her face which revealed too much. But she felt transformed as if through a tear in something paper-thin was this view already imagined, half expected. Gradually he had stopped and she could hear him breathing hard behind her. And then very gently he parted the hair at the nape of her neck. It was an unexpected thing and made them suddenly awkward with each other, and Anna, gauche, swollen-eyed, got clumsily to her feet, and fled. To hide away in her own room.

*

Irrepressible, light as air, the children poured out of school on their last day; it was an exercise on the dominance of the gene – much on her mind – as parent found child, and Anna saw her daughter come towards her with her father's frown. Nick, trailing his gym bag behind him in the dust, suddenly streaked away with some of his friends, leaving Fay behind. How the summer stretched in front of them.

'Can we go away somewhere?'

'What with?'

'Money! All that money that Hideo gives you.'

How can it cost so much? wondered Fay after Anna had spelt out their situation; and Nick, who had been called sharply back, complained that day trips were no fun, his face already screwed tight with sulks: all her fault. Anna briefly considered the image of a raging young Hideo confronting his mother. Their children are not reprimanded; society forces them into a mould all too soon. 'You're beastly,' Nick was saying. Other places; other manners, other habits.

There were workmen moving in opposite, and Dorothy, who Anna rarely saw, confirmed the house was being got ready for sale, there was no one in it. So, no more of Dave and Janet then. Louise also seemed to have dropped out of sight, for an unknown man had answered her phone, and in an unfriendly voice thought she'd gone to New York, and didn't know when she'd be back. All Anna's friends were winging off independently for the summer.

*

The weather was turning hot. Early that morning, alerted by the sight of a clothes moth, Anna had at last taken out Gregory's remaining clothes. She held them briefly to her; a faint, very faint ghost of a smell came from them, then disappeared in the morning air. Two postcards of the same blue sea and the same sort of cliffs, though from different places: from Michael, and from her parents. Yes, England's safe, picking up the newspaper and seeing through the window the children at some game on the grass (Hideo was not yet up). The breeze was heavy with honeysuckle. Turning to the overseas page, at the bottom in scarcely more than fifty words (much less than for the description of the island meeting) it stated briefly that the police in Tokyo and Kobe were on full alert. A gang killing at the weekend. Two men gunned down.

'I am not to return. I stay in England my father says.'

'Did he say why?'

Why had this feud been reported? Guerrilla movements in South America, possible coups in Africa, the plight of dissidents – all carried within their stories an internal logic; the right to be informed existed in such accounts. This carried no logic. All one could suppose was that the rise in influence of Japanese business, their apparent inscrutability made even this important. Or were they seen as a threat? Journalists also intrigued by their paradox.

'Very important that no one lose face. If a man lose face he will be angry, and will revenge himself, then fresh revenge follows that.' Hideo spoke as if he had worked on the words. He went on: 'But I do not understand one thing. I think they always prefer it looks like accident, not this shooting. That is bad.'

It took Anna some time to understand that it was bad because the killing was crudely done. It had been messy. She felt betrayed. The previous night she'd felt so close to him; now again in a process of alienation, images passed to and fro across her mind; things once seen cannot easily be forgotten, and episodes once read cannot be put back into a book. Terrible things had been done in the name of this quiet country, she thought angrily, and here he is concerned over the inelegance of a murder! No wonder we cannot understand these people.

Where had Otaki been standing? To whom was he making his bow? Whose side could he be on? But neither could remember; they hadn't watched with sufficient care.

Nothing any more that she'd read or seen helped to resolve what had happened or was likely to happen. Sometimes she could not believe that anything could be amiss, for the summer was magnificent, everyone agreed . . . and after that appalling winter . . . but she was uneasily aware how the road was emptying of neighbours and that made her nervous, for they were the familiar between her and that worrying presence outside, which lingered still, though on the edges of her consciousness. Sometimes as she locked the door at night and double-checked, her hand would stay on the key, and she seemed to hear the soft padding about in the dark.

The news that Hideo's course was finished jolted Anna:

'You didn't tell me there were no more lectures at college!'

The fine eyes, not really almond-shaped, looked at her in a new way. She flushed, and persisted: what of his London friends, the ones he went drinking with (the ones, she wanted to add, he spent the night with)? But it seemed one laughed, one spent the time pleasantly; 'We do things together, many of us together. Not like you, one special friend and just one time together. Jolly good fun.' He seemed defiant.

'I think one friend is sad,' Hideo was saying at Clare's. She had reasoned smoked salmon is raw fish, but he was eating it with far too little respect, refusing lemon, and spreading it with horse-radish sauce. Richard, Clare's husband, found this amusing, and Clare took it in good part; ah, but you see, she explained, patiently choosing her words with care, we feel that only a few people can fully understand any one person, and so we have close and not-so-close friends, and after that there are neighbours and colleagues.

Hideo, in the act of shoving in more salmon, appeared genuinely bemused.

'People are individual, after all, although of course we are the same in many ways, fundamental ways, I mean,' she went on in some desperation; her look showed she was beginning to follow some of Anna's bewilderment.

'We are different, I think.' His face was flushed.

'From each other, of course. That's what I've been saying.'

There was silence of misunderstanding.

Anna interpreted: he means the Japanese are different.

Richard put in at this point his theory on individual differences which were less than one might suppose, being largely a matter of taste and cultural accident; and went on to elaborate about genetic codes and environment which got them all confused.

'Hideo believes that the Japanese as a race are different from all the rest.' Her eyes were fixed on him, saying: but you are an individual among your countrymen, and different from them, and you won't admit it.

Two things happened simultaneously. Richard rose with the wine bottle, and Anna's gesture of refusing wine for Hideo was seen, and Richard lifting his eyebrows at this, looking at his wife, coincided with her hand helping Hideo to cream, while smiling at Anna: don't mother the young man, meeting

119

Hideo's horrified refusal in mid-air, so that everything crashed together.

The main purpose of the evening it turned out after everything had been cleaned up, was whether Anna would like to borrow the family cottage, everyone else going elsewhere. 'And we only lend it to friends, and it's a good idea for the place to be lived in, otherwise someone might decide to take it over.'

Where?

'In the Lakes.'

'There are mountains there,' Anna said to Hideo.

There was an embarrassed pause. 'It's not large,' Clare said hastily, and Anna grew hot. Richard said it was large enough, and Anna didn't have to say anything now; their three heads turned towards Hideo, sitting collected and quiet. Anna, seeing him for a moment through Clare's eyes, saw a neat Oriental with a pleasant face who had been rather a nuisance; but when he looked directly at her his face subtly shifted, so that she was keenly aware of him in the round, aware of the shape of his body, and the inside palms of his cupped hands all in one instance; and she had to look down, troubled by the thrill she found in her body.

There was a three-quarter moon as they returned with the children taken from sleep, and the air was still warm. As they paused by the front path for Nick to search for stars – a diversion to put off that moment of getting to bed – Anna listened to the creaks and rustles round her. Plants growing by moonlight.

'Rice,' Hideo said. 'Rice also. The Rice God likes the night.'

Fay was giggling. 'You've both been drinking!'

So, Anna said tersely, was that a sin?

'Who's the Rice God?' Nick pulling on Hideo's sleeve demanding and to stop him opening the door, to put on the light.

'O Inari Sama.' He swayed slightly. 'He has fox as friend.' He bent to put the key in for them, and from further down the garden there was the sharp snap of a twig or dry wood breaking. The children's heads turned momentarily; they went indoors

120

disregarding. But Anna's heart was beating painfully hard; she went inside quickly, turning the key and tugging the door to check. For some time after the others had gone to bed she walked around, calming herself, and after a while, resolved, walked, but without a torch, back into the garden. It had not been the usual night noises that had unnerved her, but the faint smell at the back of the house, now gone, of cigarettes, or the smell of someone who smoked a great deal, who had it in his hair. Come now, she was thinking, surveying the woman opposite in the bedroom mirror, what foolishness. Only in the morning did she find out how correct her instincts were. She had left washing out, there had been no wind, and one garment was caught over the line. It had been careless of the man to flip it away from his face. Perhaps he had been trying too hard not to leave footprints.

'You cannot bring shame to your family. What will they think of me? I must do as my father says. He says, stay until I myself ask.'

'But Hideo, this letter – forgive my asking – this is the first letter your mother has written to you?'

'Yes, it is the first time.'

Anna said nothing; she was beginning to learn how to use silence.

'She has put down what is in her heart.' Clearly he was troubled. What would he do?

'I must stay in England.'

Anna hardly dared breathe and told herself she must stop feeling and reacting like this at once.

'Why has she written to you? Because she is ill?'

The letter in his hand, pale blue, the ink a darker blue, the script unknown and unknowable, struck her as written in precise strokes; there was nothing distressed or frantic about it.

'Can you ring your father?'

He bowed his head. He couldn't do that.

And his friends, the ones he drank with, could they do nothing? Find out what exactly . . . or carry a message. And where had they all gone?

'Holiday?'

He wasn't being straight about this. In the same way that she had been isolated through bereavement, it also seemed to her that he was isolated through some deliberate policy, but this was such a mad idea she dismissed it. Could he go to the consulate and say he had problems . . .?

'But I do not have problems. You have problems.'

Her problem was what on earth a respectable man like Professor Otaki was doing openly mixed up with a bunch of criminals.

'He is Shinto.'

'What?'

'Maybe Buddhist.'

Exasperated, she said she didn't follow, and he watched her with a look of similar bafflement.

Several times in the night now, sleep broken, reaching into the quietness for signs of anything wrong, there never did appear to be anything wrong yet it was always hard to get back to sleep for her body seemed poisoned, or stiff as if she had been running for too long. There had been no reply from Professor Otaki; nothing more in the newspapers, nothing on the television news. From over the road the steady thrum of a cement mixer, the blast of radios, overhead the thumping of the children. There was always a part of her waiting for something to happen.

And Hideo had taken to lying. He was hopeless at it, claiming he was joining the Americans for trips when Anna knew it was impossible; he grew reckless, making wild claims for what he was going to do, until Anna for shame stopped asking. She only knew that he left the house and stayed away from it as much as possible. And this hurt.

Slowly walking down through the college grounds to meet Clare, Anna came across the summer intake of American students standing under the cedar tree for photographs; they shouted and hectored, the photographers grimaced: they were trying to capture the vitality if not happiness. It really was an easycare group. Clare laughed at her.

'Sourpuss! They're noisier, but from up here they're the same.'

Anna looked the length of the library. No one studying. 'What do I have to do to get in?'

'The key is under the outhouse tiles. And you don't even have to cut wood.'

'Pity. I'd rather like that.'

'You really ought to go, Anna.' Clare's eyes were concerned. 'You're a bit worn out, aren't you? I've been meaning to say,' as she sorted out papers, 'everyone gets neurotic at times. I mean, the cat scratches, you think fleas, you powder the cat, but you go on seeing the fleas. That's like you and these Japanese. You know what I mean?'

'No.'

'I'll put it another way: we're a mixed society, aren't we? We got a Chinese takeaway the other day but I didn't stand there saying to myself, My God, these are Chinese: beware of Fu Manchu.'

Anna laughed but pointed out that this was because Clare was not obsessed. 'And *I* am, and with cause. And I worry about Hideo.'

'You don't know much about him though, do you, not really. What does he do? Where does he go? You don't know.'

'Are you trying to tell me he's untrustworthy?'

'Richard and I liked him, Anna. There's something very attractive about him. Perhaps there are things he . . . Oh, I don't know. But I begin to think they are very different.'

Anna felt she might be trapped into saying the wrong thing.

'Take the children and get away. It's been hard for you. Go and see something different. You'll come back a changed woman.'

'Perhaps I will. And it really doesn't matter?'

'Not at all. And there isn't a phone.'

Returning back past the shops – even Betty had gone away for her week in Wales – Anna checked at the sight of her children who had drifted with that natural attraction towards muddle across the road and into the builders' sand. And why it should hit her now rather than the other times, she couldn't say – perhaps the brain has to freewheel for a while to work better – but she stopped at the back door and examined it inside and out. All that had bothered her at the time had been the broken panel, and they had been so sure of the horrifying explanation. Now she asked if the lock had been tampered with, but of the many scratches around the panels she could guess nothing, for it had been mended. She cursed herself for simply not paying attention.

'Will you come?'

Tower of London or Hampton Court. The children stood dutifully by; for them it was a toss-up between the Bloody Tower or the Maze – they knew the ice-cream was to be had at both.

Tails. The Palace then. Turn tail and run. She would tell him on that neutral ground that she had to get away.

They were walking through the rose-garden, the children ahead. 'Could you go to a hotel perhaps?' (What was she hoping for?)

In this enclosed space, the roses in their proper place, docketed and just summer-pruned, sent little puffs of perfume over the walks, the unimportant sparrows hopping freely below them.

He had said nothing. Anna kept her peace; there was plenty to look at, and as they moved into the main avenue the coaches were setting down the tourists.

It was no surprise, indeed to be expected on a warm summer weekend, that among the other visitors there should be the Japanese, however far they had to come. They were getting neatly down to form an orderly group at the foot of the bus, soberly and discreetly dressed in their town-viewing clothes – at least this Anna surmised from the uniformity of their turn-out, as if it had been agreed beforehand. She was struck by their generally short stature, but they were for the most part elderly; Hideo, being of the younger generation, was taller, and, she was thinking, he was that rare thing: a truly handsome man.

He said suddenly, 'Where are the children?' sounding alarmed, and she looked at him, wondering why he asked, and saw him staring fixedly ahead. Her heart lurched.

But Hideo had already moved with that sudden surprising swiftness. Anna was never likely to forget the man who called at the house, nor the shaming depth of her immediate and unreasonable dislike. For he was also striking to look at, except for those eyes so out of scale in his face. As before he was elegantly dressed. She stood where she was – she would not join them – watching the formality of their greeting with relief until she saw them both smile and her heart sank. Was it this man who had been going around with Hideo before? If so then his influence was to be deplored, she said to herself, and she could feel her face tightening.

They could not talk for very long, for clearly, whoever he was, he was to be of some use to the visiting party who were patiently waiting. Hideo waved his hand to her – somewhat imperiously she thought. Reluctantly she started to join him but he had already drawn away so that they could overtake the Japanese now obediently lining up for the ticket office. The man showed no sign of knowing her, but he kept his small eyes on her, and when they reached the Boleyn gateway she turned quickly round and saw he was watching them still.

'What is he doing here?'

'Oh, he is a friend.'

'Yes. But what is he doing here?'

'He earns some money taking visitors. He talks good English.'

'I know.'

'Hoh?'

'I've already met him. He came to the house.'

He said nothing more until they passed through the ticket barrier, and the children once more raced ahead.

'How came to the house?'

'He came asking for you. I don't like him,' she added, and influenced perhaps by the surroundings they were moving through, 'He is not honourable.'

They were walking up the stairs to the Wolsey Apartment when a thought struck her: was he one of the ones who had the car that time? 'Is that why you asked about the children?'

'*Hai.*'

On the walls the swords, the rapiers, the short knives, instruments that could damage and cut, were arranged as petals in flowers of shining blades.

'What is his name?'

'Sado.'

Anna gave a little snort of amusement. 'A friend, you said?'

But he walked away, pretending to be pulled by the children's insistence, forcing Anna to follow after.

*

There was an imposing black limousine parked outside her house. It had tinted windows and she could see only that there was a man with his back to her sitting alone, but as she went in by her front path, the side gate – which she'd left unlocked for the children – opened and an oriental man in chauffeur's cap came out. He grinned, and sauntered past her leaving her gaping at the impudence, and she was considering what best to do when she heard the car door and felt someone approaching as she stood fixed, holding the doorkey, facing her own front door.

Professor Otaki: somewhat less unhealthy-looking, and much better dressed.

He had not improved in memory. And she felt now that he had brought the art of politeness to such a pitch that each courteous action was a subtle insult. Thus he bowed now, any antagonism he might feel well masked, but it was experienced as a sneer. 'I am grateful you welcome me again to your charming house.'

It had never been in Anna's nature to be rude or even very outspoken, but her feelings could overrule her head, and after what she had discovered . . . 'I don't in fact welcome you. I'd far rather you turned around and got back in your car.' She flushed, hearing herself.

He hesitated only momentarily, but his demeanour changed abruptly. He was curt.

'I think you like causing trouble, Mrs Dean.'

Her protest, which had risen from some unexamined area, an almost automatic response, she stifled; she'd have to be much more careful than this. (Had he ever received that letter she'd written?)

127

She motioned him with reluctance into the house and towards a chair, but he seated himself instead at the desk. Ashtray, please, taking out a notebook.

'Hideo Ishida must return to Japan. You must give him message.'

Anna's stomach lurched. One thing to tell oneself, another to be told. But defiance was growing; suppose Hideo wanted to stay? He was young, but old enough to make his own decisions, he liked it here, he had freedom here, he should not be pushed around . . .

'I'll not be your messenger.'

Otaki pulled out a handkerchief, turned his head aside and blew. She knew enough now to see this as offensive. What was it about Hideo that made this situation possible? Something was missing. Why try to bully her, why damage her when Hideo was what they wanted?

'We have a saying in Japan, Mrs Dean: the nail that sticks out gets banged. You do not have the correct attitude. It is unhealthy.'

'Attitude to what?'

'The situation.'

'He was sent here. If it was all right to send him here, why is it wrong for him to stay?'

'Something that was good in the beginning is bad when it has no further use. That is our way.'

With an abrupt gesture she stood up, about to tell him what she knew, but movement acted as restraint. The way I've been treated, she said (surprised at her calm coldness) shows that people are not in control of what they are doing no matter what you say. I've been kept in the dark. Expected to be more than I bargained for. And then blamed – is that what it is? – and subjected to cruel tricks. But that was really childish – and why (and here she put all her scorn into her voice) it isn't even efficient – trying to send, or pretending to send poisoned sweets – and those stupid letters . . .

Otaki leant forward intently – today he was showily

128

dressed, his cuffs, white and crisp, she saw now had expensive cuff-links. The long sallow face, the prominent teeth, seemed perverse, but the whole man spoke of intelligence. He frowned.

'We sent no letters, no . . . other things.'

'Oh, of course not, and you haven't spied on the house.'

He was studying her with cold detachment as if she was an obstacle in his path. 'We have been observing the house, of course, but we sent no letters.'

Who then? What of the newspaper cuttings, the parcel, the signs . . . She described them. She'd already written about them.

His mouth had taken on a peculiar fixed grin which was alarming, but she realized it was a sign he was nonplussed. Then he made up his mind. 'Accept my apologies for this. The people concerned will be punished.' He frowned, clicking his teeth and writing into his notebook. He appeared confident at finding the culprits, in any case dismissing the subject.

'Who sent you? Who are you working for, Mr Otaki?' She wondered now whether he ever had been a professor; he'd looked the part at the time.

A sigh escaped him, and he got to his feet, dusting ash off his trousers.

'Why not just take him back,' she asked, sarcastic, 'if he's that valuable, or isn't that the "Japanese Way"?'

'He must come by himself.'

She tried again. 'He's old enough. If he wants to live his own life – '

'Not possible. His life belongs to others.'

This silenced her. Incredibly it seemed he was going to leave. She wanted to ask more, probe more, to find out . . .

'So it depends on me?'

'You? You are unimportant.'

To be bullied, and not to have anything resolved enraged her. She shouted out, what was so damn special . . . but couldn't go on.

Otaki didn't answer at once, as though checked. 'We are Japanese,' he said in a voice she thought had wonder in it, as if saying something so true, so demonstrably obvious that like the existence of the sky, the earth, it could not be explained, it simply was. 'We are unique. We are pure people. For two thousand years we have been uncontaminated. You see what happens when you mix blood. You become mongrel, and you have laziness, criminality. People should take their right place in the world. Women like you do not know your place. You have been very bad influence.'

'That's racism,' she said in growing horror at the way he was talking.

'We live in different times.' At the door, turning, 'Tell me, who has won since the war? You, or us? Those who have won are right. Remember that, Mrs Dean. That is why Hideo Ishida will return. And ask yourself: if we do not protect, what then?'

'I will come with you.'

Anna couldn't reply.

'Can I come with you? It is a good idea. Lake District is beautiful.'

'What about your racy friends?' Her voice was tart, but in fact hope, or some emotion, was causing something in her to dance.

His hands came out in that curious gesture as if he was smoothing creases out of paper, and then one hand crept up behind his neck, making him look for a moment doubtful. He did this when bewildered. He turned and went away towards the window, lifting his head to watch the swifts who were scooping insects rising at dusk. Anna followed each move with her eyes; he had such grace.

130

He straightened his shoulders and turned back to her. An authority she hadn't seen before sat on him. 'We go tomorrow.'

'So soon?'

His back to the window, the fading sun outlined his body. Anna's skin was tingling from the sun, she felt the flush in her cheeks. Something appeared to be decided. They smiled at each other.

'At once, Anna San.'

No one said much. She'd said it would be a surprise, it would be unknown, but two hours out on the motorway when Hideo had still said nothing and she was beginning to tire with the concentration needed, she asked had he warned anybody, had he said anything? And when he said he'd just left, she rejoiced. Good. He was at last breaking free, he was standing up for his right to live his own life. She said so.

She could feel him looking at her. That is not the Japanese way.

Who cares? Reckless, she remembered there was no telephone. She was glad.

They had pulled in to a service station, and were sitting in a frog-green eatery where plants sprouted and a fountain played. Only the water was real. Hideo admired the place, and Anna, not for the first time, queried his taste. He had spoken again of his mother. He had been almost smothered with love; clearly he was very close to her, almost in awe. She eyed him. Yes, his mother was jealous, possessive; was she angry with the father? Her anxieties were well founded, for Anna began to see how Hideo could be cast off from the island fortress and never be able to get back in.

131

She had been fiddling with the car keys, and he had looked over the children's shoulders at the route. Now he took the keys from her, let her get into the car herself, though carefully checked the children's doors, and they drove off in silence. The flatlands were building up into hills, and the climb beginning that would bring them into Lakeland. The sun was out, the children asleep; Anna settled into her seat. He was a good driver. Sitting at her side he was taller, his body long, she noticed, and his hands resting on the wheel stirred her deeply; she was protected and for the first time felt secure and no longer needing always to be on her guard. She went back in her thoughts to the first few days after his arrival, and could not credit the difference. How could she have thought him childish?

'Did you bring your passport?'

He turned quickly. 'I bring everything.'

He was after all only a few years, a very few years younger. When a police car overtook them and they were cautioned about speed, he laughed. In the films there is always a big chase, and the driving is very exciting. He liked that.

Anna said she didn't like thrillers, you know.

Again he laughed. 'I cannot say that word.' Then he asked, 'Why do you always say "you know" when I do not know? Do you know what I feel?'

She was astonished and couldn't say a thing.

'I like to learn,' he said, 'everything.'

'Are you quarrelling?' Fay asked from the back.

We are, Anna was thinking, turning to look away towards the high wall of hills. Soon they would be going through the pass, from here its entrance still hidden. Have we got as close as that?

Not to worry. Was that what he'd said? She pressed her hands between her knees.

*

132

The house had its back to the mountains and the rear garden sloped steeply uphill from the walls, so steeply that the lowest branches of an apple tree near the house were level with the eaves. It was sturdily built, with a heavy oak door and small windows set into thick walls. Hideo had parked the car on the only bit of level ground, and was looking away from the house towards the lake some twenty yards distant. They had driven in increasing delight through the empty roads, mounting higher and higher, and then followed the route through woods which climbed steeply along the side of Skiddaw. There had been spiders under the slates of the outhouse where Anna cautiously felt with her fingertips for the keys. She heard the sound of rushing water very near as she wheedled the keys loose, and the moist smell of mosses and something sweet tickled the nostrils, making one breathe deep. She did not know where they were, not even the name of the lake, and she liked it that way.

There were two eras caught in the bunch of keys: the old hand-crafted iron, made to turn a heavy lock, and the small intricate-toothed Yale. As the door opened, a smell made of mustiness, and herbs and split wood came with it, the children pushing past Anna as she took in the huge fireplace, the rag rugs, the pieces clearly bought in local sales. A mouse had visited the sink, but the cupboards were not spoiled. She pottered about, happy, following the instructions for turning on the water, the calor gas; and opening the back door, found the source of the noise of water, for a small stream passed along the boundary of the garden, falling over stones and going on down to the lake where Hideo still stood. The sun was setting and it lit the floor with a rosy glow. The silence

133

was filling with small noises as if things native to the place were moving back now the car engine had stopped. Peace began to settle on her like an immense soft blanket; she began to feel very tired, bone-tired, as if she had not slept for weeks. There was food to prepare.

'Can we have the end room?'

The house was long and narrow. She had merely observed that some interior walls must have been removed to make the sitting-room such a generous length, but upstairs it was clear the place was not big. The bedrooms were a good size, but there were only two of them. Another had been made into the bathroom. 'He could sleep there.' Nick pointed at a strange place in the eaves where a mattess was fitted into the triangular space where the roof met the floor.

Don't be silly.

'There's lots of beds in our room,' Fay said. 'We can change around every night. I like this place.'

Hideo would have to sleep downstairs in the main room. Down by the lake he had not moved. But then, as if he felt her eyes on him, he slowly turned and walked towards them. Seeing the oriental face before her, the lake and the mountains behind gave a sideways slip, turning briefly into a view by Hiroshige; but as he drew nearer the whole scene settled into an English familiarity, and anchored itself.

He did not mind the arrangements at all. Tranquil, he sat cross-legged on the couch.

Before the children went to bed they all walked down to the water. There was no moon, but the stars shone with such brilliance, one could see where to put the feet. The air was cool now with some damp coming from the water, and even sitting after the children had gone upstairs Anna continued to shiver, telling herself it was fatigue. It was also a constraint, for she could sense a heavy, dense quiet from the nature surrounding the house, making her realize how she fidgeted in her town-house, doing the small chores, constantly on the move; and here, where there was no longer

134

anything to do, her hands felt worse than idle, they felt full of nerves. Was this a mistake?

As if he knew and was unmoved by it, with the same quiet competence Hideo began to lay the fire.

'Where did you learn to do that?'

'At my grandparents' home. They lived in the north. It is very cold there.'

'Your mother's parents? You said they sent her away.'

'To become geisha, yes.'

When the wood caught they sat together not speaking, watching the flames.

'I shall have to sleep,' she said, getting up into her role of guardian of the house and the people in it.

'I lock the door,' he said.

She had taken the iron key from the shelf near the door and he took hold of the other end, shocking her, for the iron from cold was suddenly charged and warm. She gave a little snort of surprise, her fingers tingling, hastily began up the stairs, and then remembering her responsibilities and past experience: 'You will be careful with the fire?'

He bowed, smiled. '*Hai*, Anna-San.'

Anna crawled into the big, soft bed. Its previous occupants must have always lain very close together, for there was a pit in the middle. She lay on her stomach, burying her face into the singing pillow.

Hideo was again standing at the lake edge when Anna looked out in the morning. The sky was pale blue with a few clouds, rounded and flat bottomed, which began to break up and float away separately over Skiddaw. She was about to call when a stone whipped past her, breaking the calm and the surface of the water. She saw Hideo stiffen and spring round, but when he noticed it was Nick he grinned boyishly.

The day was spent exploring for they were unwilling to go near a town. And the children running naturally ahead, the two adults went silently along the path through the woods rising behind the house. As the rocks began, something about them made Hideo stride ahead of her, causing Anna again to suffer a sense of being displaced and in another country, until a walker, solid in orange anorak, hove round a bend: a man who hardly noticed them, who passed, eyes fixed on some firm point for his tread in front of him.

'We must find the children.'

She was soothed by the surroundings, murmuring it was all right, and minutes later they came upon the children at the waterfall. It fell in a fine line of white from high above them. A faint mist hung from it, landing lightly on the face; and where it hit the ground it surged passionately round the boulders, covering their brown with a silvery skin of water. Above the sound of water was the call of birds. The great peace was stealing over Anna. Why hadn't she realized how she held herself twisted, as it were, away from the world, her body knotting tight from fear? This realization coming to her before the waterfall made her feel suddenly battered and aching. She left the others to go on and returned through the gentle trees alone, throwing off the mental load with each step until she came to the haven of the house, and lying down, tipped, as if anaesthetized at last from pain, backwards into deep sleep.

Rain came the next day with a grey thoroughness, but couldn't depress them. Hideo stood in it, hatless, waiting for the struggle into boots to be done, and Anna, pushing wet strands from her face, could see how the rain would gather and roll off his thick black hair. Why it should give so much satisfaction to toil with the wind whipping up the side of mountains, sliding and slipping, no one knew. At the top no one was about, except far away someone was perhaps exercising hounds for there was the sound of distant barking. Through the rain, Keswick below, and the outline of Derwentwater.

That night they needed a fire, they were so drenched. He had taken the wood from Anna's hands. Somewhere, struggling to get out was some prancing mischief in her throat, which could be a shout, or laughter, but as easily, tears. She stood in the doorway, away from her children in dressing gowns and Hideo in his cotton yukata kneeling at the fire. The yukata looks good on anyone; one sees why the Japanese find beautiful the nape and the shoulders, for there is something tender and breath-catching at that junction of black hair against the skin on the bending neck. Had she given something away? For he had glanced swiftly up, folded his legs beneath him, and again looked darkly at her. This wretched pulse was beating in her throat. The desire was so strong she grew afraid. See, he demonstrated how; the paper wraps the stone, the stone blunts the knife, the knife cuts the paper.

They played that game with scissors, Fay said, forming a small fist.

Anna curled her legs under her, and when they enquired shook her head; she would watch, most of all she wanted to watch. Her heart, perhaps out of condition, she reasoned, from the exertion, threatened to suffocate her. The air was too close. It would build up to a storm without doubt.

They played, forgetting her. The firelight threw random shadows. At times Hideo's face changed as he moved or the light caught it, making him intriguingly different, and then increasingly familiar. Only the children remained the same, their round, unmarked faces throwing no shadows.

137

There's going to be a storm. Listen to the rain!

Nick in particular liked storms especially if warm in bed, but Fay, drooping over the wood basket, no longer wanted to play. Without complaint they kissed their mother, hesitated, and then as if deciding something had altered, went to Hideo, and upstairs.

He built up the fire. Anna hovered upstairs, irresolute, brushed her hair without thinking. 'You've cleaned your teeth twice,' Nick said. He was taking his time.

'Why not?'

'It's not rainwater, you know.'

'Shut up. Go to bed. Go to sleep.'

The place by the fire was empty. It was almost too hot. They had not switched on the lamps so now she was seeing blindly, but he was there standing by the door.

'I came to lock up,' she said, lying.

Hideo opened the door. Anna caught her breath. The sound of the stream clear as they both looked over the lake. The lake was like creased silk. One could make out other small sounds: the water moved by wind knocking the tiny pebbles into the sedge, and owls in the woods above their heads. The cool air smelling of moss and water came round the edge of the house to the door. Anna was trembling. She went and knelt in the Japanese position in front of the fire, placing her hands in her lap. Was he still there looking at this foreign night sky, and were the spirits of place strong enough? She could feel in the huge still presence of the mountains an immense stability surrounding them; she let out a little sigh. He had moved behind her, but she herself would stay where she was until this thing was resolved. And gravely, Hideo tended the fire; the way he held things moved her deeply. With care he built the fire, layering the chips of wood along the logs. The cotton of his yukata was stretched tight over his shoulders, and taut down his back and over his buttocks, the square blue pattern folding into darts under his knees. Bending low to the floor he blew into the embers, sending sideways puffs of ash until a long tongue of flame thrust out of the timber. And he knelt formally it seemed before her so that she couldn't help a small smile. How quiet it is in the mountains. The wood in the fire was giving little clicks and soft hisses. The oriental eyes with their fine lines rested on her. She bowed down, her head touching his knees, but he lifted her, opening her gown. For a long time he looked not at her face but her body, and at her centre where the hair met the flesh in the V of her thighs; when he met her eyes, her hand reaching out for his sash, how they changed so swiftly from kneeling to lying she could never remember, only his hands parting her, and the urgency of that first coming together – Ah, this was what it was; she had almost, not quite, forgotten.

Later he rose and stood over her, and while she looked at him he still, it seemed, looked only at her thighs, getting down again to stroke her, unable to stop touching as they became desirous again; and sometime later, the fire low, she tried to leave but he wouldn't let her go and they curled united in his bed where he made love to her again slowly and languorously. Sometime again she woke hearing a wild howl on the night. They both listened. He said into her ear: 'Kitsune. Lady Fox,' and Anna felt such a power of emotion she wanted to put her head back and shout too. She put her hands into the strange thick hair, pressing her fingertips against the bone; she wanted him to kiss her.

In that early morning light she awoke, and lay uncomfortable and intensely happy. This night had led her back into a state of what she would call grace, which could not be taken away. The sleeping Hideo at her side looked no longer the compelling lover of the night before, but relaxed and smooth as a young boy. But as she tried to creep from the bed, he awoke, and catching hold of her laid her down, and while she protested, laughing, amazed, proceeded energetically to make love to her all over again.

*

139

Fay was sitting on the doorstep, her bare legs stretched to the
sun, and no, she hadn't seen Hideo that morning, and why
had she been sleeping so long, and what were they going to do
today? It was already hot.

Anna was glad the children were up before her; she didn't
know how she could face Hideo in this bright morning. The
sun lit every corner, the pink hollyhocks pressed against the
wall were ahum with bees. Nick came ahead for a towel,
running from the lake.

'So you have been swimming?' she asked shyly. Hideo was
rubbing his hair and drying his ears with that surprising
practical lack of taste he showed when blowing his nose. It
was one of the things Nick so admired in him. 'Was it cold?'
Anna was willing him to talk to her.

There was no trace of the lover of the night. After a few
shocked seconds she reproved herself for expecting something, anything indeed, at such a time. But during breakfast,
and after as they talked of what they would do, there was still
nothing, no sign, no movement. He acted as he'd acted on
that first day here: a young man confident, able to take care of
things. Alone in her room, Anna tried to calm herself. It was
unreasonable of her. Did she expect him, like an English boy
in the first flush of an affair, to cuddle and sigh? Yet that was
not it. It was an awareness of something being different that
she couldn't sense.

Still hurt, she came down to find them waiting for her in
the garden. Hideo had suggested a long expedition. To
Coniston then. She didn't intend to spoil the day with girlish
sulks, but she hadn't yet got rid of the smarting.

'I will drive,' holding out his hand for the keys. She handed them over without a word. Was he now Lord and Master?

He said, 'Look Anna-San, butterflies,' and his voice was warm and surprised.

And there were butterflies around the clumps of flowers by the edge of the stream. It had been a long time since Anna had seen so many. 'Ah yes,' she replied coolly; and he turned away.

Something about his reasons for swimming nagged at her mind, but could not overcome her stunned feelings of happiness. Yet these internal concerns were blotted out in a way she recognized all too well by another of those prosaic moments of everyday life: they got as far as the lakeside of Derwentwater before Fay was carsick. Anna was not unwilling to be obliged to walk round the shores in the shade of the trees, to be alone once more with Hideo. She felt dizzy with a suppressed passion. She knew personally what suffering was – how it is possible to live with it – but this, what could she do with this? She wanted above all to be alone with him; but he, she quickly realized even when she put questions as delicately as she knew how, did not want, or saw no need to pin down whatever meaning there was. They walked in silence while she schooled herself to swallow disappointment, and after some minutes her spirits rose in spite, for the day was glorious. The children were quickly out of sight; she deliberately held back to make the space between them greater, and when they reached the jetty she led the way along it. The water had ripples which came towards them in bands; Anna, sitting, could just dip her feet into the water where the cold soft waves tipped and tipped against her warm ankles.

'Are you happy?'

'*Hai*. Yes, I am.'

'What are you thinking of?' He was looking towards a promontory where the pines angled against the wind came down to the water.

'I am thinking of Oshima.'

141

An island. She wanted to touch him but held back. At a time like this with the barriers at last broken, any Westerner, she was thinking, would have embraced and kissed. It saddened her that they did not. He was young. And yet clearly not unpractised. She would wait for the end of the day. Amazed at her total lack of guilt.

'It is very beautiful here.'

'Yes. Are you pleased?'

'I am very pleased. The children are gone long time.' He got to his feet. He seemed always now to feel guilt about the children.

They were all right. She did not want her children.

'No!' he said making her start with surprise. 'We must search for them.' As if insisting she continue to be a good mother.

'Here it is safe. Very safe.'

'Mountains are not safe.'

'Only if one is on the heights, fell-walking.' But he was already going.

They were in the next cove, skimming stones into the water. Further off was a group of lake birds, and her mind went disturbingly to the time they had taken him in the snow to the park lake. Again Anna stood back, admiring the supple bend of his body as he weighed a stone in his hand. Paper wraps stone. Should they go, or return? He wanted to go. They would go therefore.

They stopped somewhere along a coppermines road above Coniston to eat lunch and consult the map, for although Nick didn't see any hazards, Anna had taken in the uncompromising look of the Coniston Old Man. It was going to be tougher than she imagined; her instinct was against going, but with the sun out and sky clear what could go wrong? The children were reading out names impossible for Hideo, and giggling at his attempts at 'thwaite', and 'ghyll', and Fay little-know-all said they were Viking – 'You know, bad samurai' – and they went together ahead, laughing, up the track past the old

142

coppermines. At the word samurai, Anna again had that mind-slip where she saw for a few seconds the land before them transformed through strangeness into something almost alien, and she wondered how he saw it, pacing easily in a foreign land; impossible for herself, walking in similar circumstance in far-off Japan, ever to lose the sense of being away from home. He must always carry it with him.

They zigzagged up increasingly difficult rock, resting frequently, and it seemed to Anna that when they sat Hideo was nearer the children, turned slightly away from her.

'Do you like this?' Her voice, claiming him. He turned back to her, his eyes away from the sun a fathomless black. He was solemn. 'Will there be a cairn?'

'Oh yes, there must be.'

'So . . . desuka . . . It is good they have to make the stone offerings there.'

Too late Anna realized he had misunderstood. She gestured helplessly; as the wind grew stronger near the top, her words were whipped away and lost.

Look. Far away the lake, and farther still another like a drop of mercury, and further on, dimmer in a haze, what looked like sands beyond the woods and fields leading into the sea. The sun beat on their faces, but when they turned their backs all one could see ahead was a range of mountains, lit and deeply shadowed; somewhere beyond the nearest was their own. Safe at its base, the house.

But ahead and to the north-west, the land fell sharply down into a combe and rose on the other side to higher crags. It was a very old land, and deep in the shadow was menacing, deceitful.

'This is not a good place.' His head swivelled as he slowly followed the contours.

'What are all those mountains?'

'I don't know. Don't bother me, Fay.'

'The wind's too rough for this map.'

Nick said they should shout, Fay, and see what happens.

No, Hideo said firmly. It was not good for the Kami, the gods.

'Do the gods live here?'

'Of course. The gods live in the mountains.'

'But this is England.'

'These are big mountains. You can feel the gods, can't you?'

They fell silent, looking around doubtfully, but trusting this firm voice as though convinced, after glancing once more down into the dark combe, they turned away.

Here in the wind her exhilaration grew. One was free up here, free at last of the different fears that had dogged her days. She had been too much alone, she'd been too proud trying to do without help. It even felt that she had been slightly mad, that the unexplained happenings were part of a neurotic woman's heated fancies. They had no part here. She dismissed them, and laid a stone in Gregory's memory at the next cairn. As she straightened up, Hideo also adding his stone clapped his hands, bent his head, clapped again, then at last looked at her. There was harmony between them. It was the right thing to have come. As before there was that subtle change; something had been settled for him on the mountain. Though she could not read anything in his eyes, she knew, and was elated.

Then she noticed how pale Fay had become. They descended immediately, making their way over the crags, Hideo lifting Fay down to Anna, after several yards suddenly hitting scree, and Nick went over his head, slipping down in a flurry of sliding stones. The map slipped with him, and Hideo went crabwise to collect it. The tarn at the bottom was the one they'd passed before; Anna thought it different. With one child wedged in a rock, and another bleeding below on a slope of grey vicious flakes that threatened to send him tumbling into the dark grey water, why did it matter whether it was one unwelcome tarn or another? Hideo said it is dangerous country, as if speaking aloud a fact they'd agreed on and taking Fay on his back, carefully planting his legs, he began

144

the slow forwards and sideways descent. Nick, uncomplaining from fear and gripping his mother's hand, slid and bumped his way with her to the edge of the tarn where a stream fed into it. Here the land fell away in a harsh gouge towards the plain below, and Anna watched helplessly as Hideo tenderly washed Fay's face. She herself cleaned the worst of Nick's grazes, aware of a curious sympathy somewhere over these reverses of nature. But their progress was very slow. Out of direct sun the temperature was dropping. Now one could see more clearly where the crags ended at the beginning of the scree which plunged down to the deep water. It made Anna shudder. A bad accident had been barely avoided. The blame hers, because of her preoccupation.

Somewhere further down, at last they found the old track and, reassured, followed it to some old mineworkings. It was while they were standing peering from the rough verge down into one of the deep holes that Anna saw Fay naturally put her hand in Hideo's, and he kept it there. In an ugly mood, Anna dragged Nick further down the track, protesting, and she continued inwardly to rage until they reached a bridge with a fall of water. There at last she stopped, and sitting on the ground, her head pressed onto a stone, wished she could weep, dry-eyed, jealous.

'Certainly not, Fay. We've had enough for one day.'

'Then what shall we *do*?'

'Well . . . play games and things until it's time to go to bed.'

'We could go for another walk.'

'We've had enough walking. Besides it will get dark.'

'We could go for a walk in the dark.'

Anna was not going to lose her temper. 'You don't want to be sick again,' she warned, but pleasantly.

'It's cooler now.'

Anna was not to be budged. Hideo was bathing, and she didn't want to risk his hearing her getting angry again with the children. She turned her attention to books, hoping to divert them, conscious of the coming night, and the banging of her heart. Desire weighted her as if she was walking through swamp.

Other people's books are always an odd mixture. Here among the usual paperbacks, detective novels and books on fell-walking, was one on watercolour painting, and flicking through she found examples of Chinese ink wash, of trees and mountains. 'That's very like Japanese painting.'

'It's very empty,' Nick said.

'They pick out the important parts.'

'There's a lot of space around it.' He found it dull. 'Where's the rest? The rest of the view?'

'It's the way they do it. You put in the bit you can't see for yourself.' The unseen and unstated were more emphasized in this picture than the mountain itself, and something tugged at her mind, asking for attention; but she ignored it.

And Hideo, sitting by the fire after his bath, took the paper and drew a few quick lines which did not satisfy Fay. She insisted on words. For some time Anna was engrossed in titles, and when Nick curled beside her she put her hand absently on his head until she caught sight of his book and hastily placed her hand on the cover: it showed two slit-eyed yellow soldiers disembowelling what she assumed to be an American. One looked in books. How else was one to find things out? She frowned furiously at him and thrust the book spine first back into the shelf, moving to the fire as if to hide what they'd done.

Her mind on pictures, she saw one now: Fay in her nightdress, leaning all too languorously against Hideo. Dusk had come unremarked, and the firelight lit Fay's face and the hank of hair touching his shoulder; she was giggling softly and, as if expecting her mother's judgement, sent a look of defiance, tossing the hair back from her flushed face. And as if he too sensed some thing, some division, Nick pressed against Anna. Could he, he pleaded, get her hairbrush and brush her hair? It was something he'd done, which he liked to do, which had been subtly comforting in the months after Gregory had died.

Not now. Another time. Knowing she was denying him.

'Fay!' she called out sharply. 'You must not bother Hideo like that.'

'He likes it.'

Anna was firm. After the day they'd had they should go to bed in good time. She tried not to remember how she'd kept them up with her so many times out of loneliness.

Hideo had stopped drawing, but Fay hadn't moved; or shrunk if anything closer. 'No! I won't.' The face in the gloom was no longer that of a child, and Anna was chilled by the sharp cut of her voice. Inside, her spirit faltered before the woman in her daughter. And the room seemed big and charged with uncomprehended desires.

'Fay!' She spoke sharply and stood up. Fay gave a little cry and cowered towards Hideo who in his turn got to his feet. Shadows leapt about the room. He held Fay to him.

'I won't go,' Fay said again. Her head was against the opening of Hideo's yukata. Something akin to murder in her heart, nerves raw with feeling, Anna was acutely aware of the flickering light, the noises of the burning wood, the dust smell of the rag rugs, the stream outside, the wind and their breathing overlaying one another in a kind of dissonance.

And it was Nick who broke into this with the tired ordinary voice of the small boy defeated by adults, a deep sigh of resignation. 'Oh come on, Fay, we might as well.' So that Fay, shrunken and diminished now into a girl, ran to join him at the foot of the stairs, but once there went back to Hideo, kissed him, then fled without any other sign to her mother.

147

Anna had tears in her eyes. 'I'm sorry.'

Not to worry.

Neither of them moved. For whatever malign spirits might be about had not yet left. Slowly, heavily, Anna went towards the fire. The silence emptied of everything. Anna would rather have anything but silence. Silence was absence; it was the grave; it was to be alone.

'Talk to me.'

'I have not the words.'

'Try.'

'I think it is too . . . difficult.'

'I don't understand you. You must talk to me so that we can understand each other.'

'I understand you.'

'You do? How can you?'

'I feel here.' He patted his stomach. '*Haragei.*'

She was disappointed. 'Oh, sex, you mean.'

He laughed. 'That is different.'

Anna's legs were threatening to let her down. She sat and stared into the fire as if its random movements could give shape to her mind. Over by the door the room was in obscurity; she didn't want a lamp. Hideo was more yellow, more like ivory in the light of the fire.

'What is the Japanese for love?'

'*Ai.*'

'*Ai*. It sounds as if one is in pain. "Love" is a soft, lovely word.'

Again he laughed. 'Not to me. It sounds like dog bark.'

Anna managed a little smile at this. 'Oh Hideo!' Tears were running down her cheeks.

'Anna-San, I have offended you.' It was a statement.

'How can you have offended me?'

He didn't reply. After a while he began to talk of his mother. Anna was a good mother too, she was good to her children, but hard. Anna didn't want to talk of his mother, wanting no other woman here even in spirit. If he wanted to

148

talk, tell her rather of his father. She knew nothing of him apart from that voice.

His father was businessman. What sort of man, she prompted. Is he kind, remembering Hideo had once written: my father is stern.

He bent his head as if searching in there for some clue, and not finding an answer was again taking refuge in saying nothing. He is strong man.

'Physically, you mean? Or mentally?' A pause. 'Is he a big man?'

No, not big. Just strong. A man who didn't talk much.

Anna had a mental picture of the father, Kuneo his given name, getting up now on the opposite side of the world in his western-style apartment. That he looked like Hideo, but was more powerfully built. A strong man. It was he who, as Hideo reluctantly admitted, had insisted that the visit to England should take place. He had obeyed. There didn't seem to have been any choice in the matter.

Outside, Anna could hear the stream flowing. She was asking too many questions and making a gulf between them. Waiting for the children to be asleep.

'Do you like it here?'

Yes. He liked it a lot.

'With me?' She regretted the words as soon as they were out.

'With all of you.'

Scrutinizing his face in the firelight, she found it hard to read anything there. Was it equally hard for him? She insisted: 'Do you like it here with me?'

She changed so much. 'You get angry one minute, laugh next minute; next by next.' And as she began laughing, he added, 'I like your big eyes, and your nose.'

'Ah I know, you Japanese call us hairy, and ugly as goblins.'

He moved swiftly across the space between them. 'I like your red hair. Anna, I want.'

149

They would go to Keswick, then Grasmere. This Anna had decided standing at the open door in the cold early morning after Hideo had gone for his swim. The mountain reflected in the water a dark grey shadow, steady and unwavering. There was some large bird making use of the lateral of air high up, level with the crags. They had been getting too inward-looking, so she was considering, soothed by love-making, and the vengeful ghosts of last night disappearing. The mist which still caught down near the water-line would go. The day would be fine.

Hideo drove. And he would pay. He would pay for everything. With Anna remonstrating, he took out far more than they could possibly need, for he wanted to buy things, he wanted to give presents; and although her money from the college came through with regularity he discounted this as if they were under his protection. There'd been other Japanese in earlier, the cashier noted, passing back the passport. He meant it pleasantly. The Lakes were popular. Leaving the others at the sweet-shop, Anna sauntered away to the tourist centre. Reading without any great involvement, as she didn't intend to visit old houses, her eye was caught by announcements for the forthcoming season of the hunts and the meeting of the hounds on Blencathra, information she was grateful for as sometimes, either in her sleep or just waking, she'd thought she'd heard the sound of yelping and the echoes of barks, and had wondered whether her mind would forever be haunted by foxes.

Grasmere she'd conceived of (perhaps from reading Wordsworth) as savage and isolated, but they found a gentler place, regrettably full of tourists. But they could walk and leave others behind. Again, the shops full of goods subtly angled for tourists' taste dazzled them, and Hideo wanted presents to take back. Anna agreed to meet after a half-hour; they could walk with lunch up the fell and eat at the first stretch of water. Her heart was beating at the thought of Hideo's return; to calm herself she wandered aimlessly among the growing crowds and gazed at the coaches rolling down the hill to the parking area. There were Italians, and she'd heard German as she was buying bread, and now as she watched half diverted she saw the Japanese. They were packing out of coaches, small people, some women in kimonos in drab greys and browns, others almost a caricature of the country look: homespun tweed. The men wore hats with their suits. As they descended they clustered immediately together consulting their papers; the contrast couldn't be greater from the coach at their side where European tourists were spilling out, some immediately walking off, getting in the way of cars entering. The Japanese women interested Anna. She observed them tugging their dress, straightening the fold of the kimono over the breast, smoothing it at the knees. The men corrected their hats, adjusted waterproofs over their arms, looked round amiably. Her amusement had to be for herself alone. One could not expect Hideo to be diverted. But he would have noticed the French, long limbs thrown out, heads turning to gesture, so tenuously together, and moving off as individuals to conquer the town.

Why did they come? And so far? Was it imagination to see this group as more than country based, or were they indeed dressing to conform to surroundings? Anna, asking herself why she wanted so badly to travel, could answer easily: to get away from her suffocating and restricted life; to find difference; to forget responsibility; to escape. Surely that was what everyone was after? Except (she was thinking) where it is a more controlled escape, as here, where they were travelling in flocks, wanting the reassurance of their own kind. Not like we Westerners, she thought, the way we shoot off at tangents.

There was something to be said for both. She observed them; a solid group acting in harmony in ways she thought she was beginning to understand. The English, acting as individuals and with a greater freedom of choice, could go all ways.

She saw the children coming to meet her where she was comfortably propped up against a warm stone wall. Hideo had dressed for the part, as Mr Lakeland Walker, and in spite of the heat had on a knitted hat and professional walking boots. He appeared to have changed his shirt.

The children were also carrying what turned out as they drew nearer with happy grins, to be small rucksacks. They had badges pinned prominently.

'You spoil them.'

'We've all got presents,' said Nick. 'See Hideo's.'

He showed the pair of binoculars, clearly expensive. Anna's present was an equally dear set of orienteering instruments which she did not have the faintest idea of how to use. Weren't they something to do with taking your bearings?

'I've been watching your countrymen. You can't get away from them.'

He stiffened, became serious. Where?

Down the street there.

He began walking away in the opposite direction. 'That is not good.'

'Don't worry. Your friends aren't with them.' She was light-hearted.

'It is loss of face to my father if stories get back to him.'

'What stories? About what you've been doing in London?'

He was scornful. 'Japanese do not care about that Soho thing.'

'And what your friends might say of me? I thought you came to the Lakes to be with me,' she said, petulant, childish.

'If it gets out, people can hold something against you.'

Stupid.

'You shouldn't have said that,' hissed Fay, for he was walking ahead, Nick running to catch up.

'What did I say?'

What had she said?

152

The contradiction in their surroundings intrigued her almost to obsession. She couldn't put her finger on what it was; the spirits of the place one felt so strongly up there on the mountains retreated almost out of sight at the house. And yet she felt watched. In the evening now the windows of the house were black, revealing nothing inside, reflecting only the branch of a tree, and the pink-flushed sky behind. She saw Hideo's hand grasp the key and put it into the lock with an accustomed gesture, turn the key, and pull the door slightly towards him before pushing it away. As if he had always done so.

And the house, empty and untouched, let out a breath of warm air through the door.

Hideo was sitting on a chair, massaging his knee, evening drink in his other hand. They had all caught the sun, and the languor from the long walk had overtaken them, leaving Anna sunk in her chair opposite, leaden limbed and unwilling to get up to cook. Inside, her heart was beating a relentless tattoo on her temples.

As it was still hot, they walked after supper down to the lake where it would be cooler. Even here the air was heavy. Thunder, perhaps. Hideo was thinking, maybe.

The animals of the night were coming to their time; as the birds higher went to roost, the bats were swooping over the water.

'Oh yes. Your mother is fox.' The children with wide-open eyes turned from Hideo to her, half alarmed. Then, laughing in the faded light, 'Because she is cunning?'

'Because she changes shape. And she is wild.'

'Changes shape?'

'Oh yes,' he said solemnly, and, bending, skimmed a stone

expertly so that it hopped once, twice, five times before sinking.

'You're teasing us, Hideo.' Their stones would not skim. 'How do they change shape?'

'Foxes change into beautiful women. Sometimes into men. They go to work. Drive cars, do everything, do business; but they are really foxes.'

'I don't believe you. When do they change?'

Another stone flew along the surface; it dropped with a scarcely audible plop. He straightened up and began moving towards the house. 'They change behind your back. Or when you are drunk, or afraid.'

Anna was thinking of hunting. Do they hunt, at home?

Frowning, he faced her. Home?

'In your own country.'

'Ahhh . . . not really.'

Oh no. How could a people who had demonstrated the beast in the last war not do so? Was it never sport to kill, for them? She felt poisoned. And then suddenly, as if it had been inserted somehow beneath the skin, why should she have recall of the rubbishy tales Nick had picked out from the book he'd found – told with an excited whisper – of finely honed blades, of weapons used skilfully and with stealth. She should be ashamed of a mind that turned things over as if rummaging in a dustbin.

'Anna!'

She was standing by the open door now that the children had gone; the night sky dense with dark grey cloud.

'Anna-San, what is the matter?'

What does one say? Between yesterday and today, what alteration that she should shrink from him as he comes towards her, and hesitates? He looks like a boy again. Apprehension and bafflement sit between them; afraid of misunderstanding, she keeps silent, while knowing that silence is the greater enemy.

It was he who broke first. 'I think you change, Anna.'

154

Outside came a sudden long sigh from the trees; it came round the side slopes of the mountain, then stopped. A smaller sigh came round the lake, followed by a long low rumble which petered out to nothing.

'The thunder's got no teeth,' she said.

'What no teeth?'

'My grandmother used to say it. When we were getting frightened, when she knew it would not be a bad storm, just a small one.'

She thought he looked relieved. Whatever it was, he took her hand. A large drop of rain fell on the end of a fern near the door, bending it down, and as the water rolled off the fern bounced upright again; another drop splattered in the middle of the path like a stain. Another and another, getting quicker.

Anna lay in the darkened room, hearing the downpour; Hideo curled on her, nuzzling at her breasts with his mouth. How could she understand him, this alien lover, she who'd not even understood her husband? Hideo also did not understand her; he understood neither the English nor himself. They were lost, but the rain made a thin curtain of protection around them. Now, above all, she wanted to be held strongly, and be comforted. Instead, she held this young man in her arms like a child at the breast. When you have children you at last realize there is no home-coming for you. You yourself, with all your frailties, all weakness, inadequacy...it is you who are home.

They'd thought it still teeming with rain when they awoke but it was the stream swollen to twice its size in the night, flowing into the garden, the earth drenched and glimmering with water. The lake held a faint steam above its surface. And other things had been brought out by the rain. On the path immense orange slugs:

'How disgusting! You wouldn't eat those, would you?'

Hideo was not paying attention. Yes.

'You would? Arghhh . . .'

She detected in Hideo an annoyance with the children this morning. And she said rather sharply that she had shopping to do, and wanted to be by herself.

Her route lay through woods of beech, clean-washed, where she stopped briefly to take in the smell of refreshed earth stirred by her feet. The trees held no menace even in shadow. How easy it was to hide in this country, with its twists and secret places. Surely they couldn't be found? The house itself was hidden, a den; no, they couldn't be run to earth.

She had picked a letter up casually after hearing the postvan stop at the box near the road, and stuffed it into a pocket. Ah, letters, here where no telephone, no radio, no television, or newspapers brought the outside world to the door, she'd forgotten . . .

Clare wrote: I met the postman while I was checking the house for you. He'd tried twice to get the special delivery to you so I signed for it and sent it on as it may be important. Everything here is dull. The town is muggy and hot. Lots of people have gone away. Remember when it used to be the French who emptied out of town? Richard and I are longing to get away – but don't worry we don't want the cottage. Stay as long as you like. We're going to France! Soon!

The envelope, strong and white, slashed across with thick blue crayon, was addressed to Anna. Inside there was merely this cryptic message: 'Tell him Oyabun asks for him,'

It was a new experience to realize concretely what it was like to have opponents of this calibre: no differences of opinion, no division because of politics or class, but a straightforward enmity. It made no more sense now than it had weeks ago. She couldn't answer why Hideo was so important to them. Were they getting at him through her? And herself? Had it been foreseen all along that she and Hideo would become – at least

156

she supposed this was the term – lovers? Now she asked if she hadn't been marked out from the very beginning, sitting there ignorant in her den, licking her children, mateless.

As she scuffed at broken fern with her feet, a keener, more focused dread began to take over: the feeling of being watched was giving way to a sense (which was far more scaring) of being known.

An insignificant summer wind was moving the tops of the trees. Impetuously she moved higher still, which brought her to a plantation. On the fringe of this she could pick up the almost inaudible sigh that comes from woody bushes in the heat. Pine woods are sad places where few birds sing. The person of Okasan came to her. What had her life become without her son, deserted for another woman by the father of that son? Was it lonely for such a woman? And why had she been so fearful, those telephone calls masking God knows what anxiety?

But I, she decided, I am going to say nothing. My mouth will stay firmly shut.

The sun set as forecast that evening in a rosy-red sky clear of clouds, and the mountains were in such deep shadow that Anna, thinking herself into the Japanese mind, could see them now not as symbols of permanence, but on the contrary, sometimes unstable, and shifting.

Yes, he liked mountains. The alps at Tateyama.

He didn't go down to the lake but stayed with her, sitting on the threshold step, his arm casually round her shoulders. 'I dreamt about you last night, Anna, because you were so strange all yesterday.'

'I dreamt about you too, because I find you strange!'

157

He laughed. 'But it was a nice dream. We were in Japan and we had taken a bath, and you were hot and wet from the bath, and your skin – '

'What sort of bath?'

'A huge bath in a great outdoor place with rocks. A spa? I know a place like that. You will like it, Anna.'

She said, 'I dreamt you were making love to me, but I was lying back watching you. You were sharpening your knife, and you began very slowly to slice pieces off me. Very lovingly,' she said into the silence. 'You were gentle. And I couldn't move.'

Here at least she knew what to do. Anna rested her head on Hideo's shoulder. Nothing would come down from the mountain. At some distance the men would wait, posing as businessmen perhaps, keeping themselves to themselves, spending money, disarming. Their politeness would be noted, their cleanliness remarked. She mused, her hand on his kneecap, at the fastidiousness: Hideo still took off his shoes on entering the house, though it was arguable that the outside was cleaner. He still scrubbed himself clean as if polluted by mere air, and she wondered again at what great struggles he'd had to make to overcome repugnance at foreign flesh. There must be, she thought, a hatred somewhere of contamination. One did not know why. A dark history.

'It is good here.'

The feeling between them was getting unbearably strong; her breath caught in her throat and she sighed deeply. His hand tightened round her shoulders.

'I do not want to return.'

Did he mean to London? Or Japan? She was not going to ask, and although it was foolish as the children were not yet asleep, although it wasn't yet dark, although the house was open to the road, they made love on the slope by the stream, concentrating wholly on each other, accepting the stones, the deep damp grass, the mosquitoes. It was different again, fulfilling, and final.

158

He said, 'I can work in America.'

She was putting calamine, first on his bites, then on hers. Was calamine tinted differently? Mosquitoes had enjoyed his clean skin.

'My father does business in America. And then you could come.'

'On a visit?'

Reality silenced them.

Crosslegged on the couch in his yukata, he rocked to and fro, 'I will not go back,' repeatedly began beating the fist of his right hand against the palm of his left.

Where had her calm come from? Why wouldn't he go back?

Gestured wide, his hands came out as if to hold up a large bowl. Here.

She walked away to the door, drawing her gown around her as if it might be cold outside, and there were the mountains, a dark black against a purple-grey sky. She turned back to look at the stranger, hoping to catch herself out, but it was no good: incongruous, and not strange enough, he was as she studied him deeply familiar, and she didn't want to let him go.

'Anna, what can I do? You know, if I go back they will have a wife, they have work for me.'

'You can say no.'

'I can say no, but it makes trouble.'

Abruptly she asked because it was in her mind, 'Does your father go to work every day?'

'Every day, early. He goes weekends as well.'

'Then he will be at his desk right now. Right this very moment in time.'

Outside there was just a slight wind in the trees; that and the water falling. They'd listened in the woods and decided on the different sounds trees make. But trees are always there.

'You see? It's because I know nothing. You know about me and about your own people. The ways of thinking really are inscrutable.'

'But we are very modern society.'

'That's not what I mean.'

'I will go to America.'

'Is it as simple as that?'

He was surprised. 'Yes, I can work in America.'

'And your father will give you a job? In America?'

'Of course. No problem.'

She smiled; what confidence, what arrogance. The British used to take beads for the natives before conquering them. You take transistors. 'I'm sorry. *Sumi masen*, Hideo-San,' she cried, pushing her head down onto his knees, 'but it's not to be simple for me.' She stayed there, waiting perhaps for his hand to light on her head. Instead he cried out, 'Okasan.'

It was too dark to see his face.

'She didn't want me to come. She tried again and again to make my father change his mind.'

'But you said he'd only adopted you recently. She has rights. How could she let him dictate . . . ?'

He didn't know the word. In any case his mind had gone far away. Okasan didn't approve of the West, or its habits. His head bowed while he talked, but Anna didn't need to be reminded of the woman who did ikebana. She was, he said quietly, very proud; proud of herself and her son, proud of being Japanese. With no real sense of what he was saying, he told how she'd been so afraid he'd meet some Western girl, and Western women were, to her, unclean.

Crouched in front of him, Anna was a suppliant. She shifted, and the smell of her body changed by love-making released around them. This ominous woman was right, her instincts correct that he would be polluted. Anna herself was

160

polluted by her growing knowledge of the way the world went. Only the foolishly ignorant or the blind innocent could escape it.

The possibility that Okasan was behind the sending of the letters receded still more. Okasan could not arrange her son's life as she arranged flowers. How could it end, that story acted out contrariwise on the other side of the world? Puzzling it through, her hands automatically gathering things together and tidying, Anna was stifled, unable to ask openly about the letter, which had clearly been posted in London – probably by Otaki.

The children played quietly, and as if from intuition did not demand to go on a walk but played near the stream. But then they began to be sulky and troublesome.

After some time Anna saw they were occupying themselves with building a dam across the stream, and when she snapped at them for getting wet, they lowered their eyes, squatting by the rocks, their backs stiff with rebellion.

'Are we going back?' Nick was asking as Anna rested for a while in the afternoon sun. She was watching the butterflies over the buddleia bush with regret.

'Tomorrow.'

'I don't want ever to go back.'

'We have to,' Fay said. 'It's where our house is.'

'We could change our house.' They talked softly over her as if they had already said it many times between themselves.

'Will Hideo go back?'

Hideo was at the open door, hearing his name, that quality of passive waiting more marked than ever. He couldn't understand her insistence, or her preparations as she moved methodically from one thing to another, passing time until the evening when they could be alone.

Some time later, after she had finished the many essential tasks and the children had gone upstairs, she at last broke the silence between them. She had not known where to begin. Her eyes were hurting; only one lamp on. It was a sultry night.

'He's dangerous, you know, Otaki.'

'Ah so . . . *desuka*.' His face was moist, as if from a fine layer of oil, and he was staring into his glass.

He said, 'I have freedom here. There is no space in Japan.'

(No longer. Not here any longer.) 'What does Oyabun mean?'

He laughed at her bad pronunciation. 'Big Boss.' He was pleased with himself for knowing. 'Top dog.'

Irony followed her everywhere. 'Oh. He asks for you.'

'Me?' He pointed the finger at himself. 'Me, he asks. Who?' Then he thought. 'Which Oyabun?'

'Which! How do I know which?'

He frowned. 'You laugh. Why?'

'There is nothing else to do.'

'Ah, Englishwoman,' seating himself, crosslegged, and reaching for more wine.

'Don't have too much. We have to think.'

He sipped gravely, waiting.

Anna felt ill-equipped on this very night to do battle with the oriental mind. Hideo, as she'd so often been reminded, had withheld facts about himself and his life, in a way she'd seen as deliberate and calculating as a calligrapher poised with his brush over the blank page: aware that the black of his statement and the white of the space around it had equal importance. The making of sense and finding the meaning had come to this: a method more intuitive, still full of dangers of misinterpretation. These shadows in his life showed up as only the faintest of lines.

He didn't talk of his father as if he knew him. Indeed how

162

ould he? Why, after all those years of ignoring Hideo, had he chosen suddenly to adopt him, take him over? Why at this particular time? A rich man, did he need a new heir?

He didn't know. Maybe it was age, or health. It was all maybe, as if he didn't know a thing.

So then, how old? Sixty-five? Ahhh . . . So he was in the war, as what, an army man, or in the navy?

In Manchuria. And the knife, he was saying, as if the two remarks came together was his father's.

Kuneo the first name. Kuneo Ishida, already forty years old, with a family of whom there remained two daughters and a wife, had taken a mistress, keeping her well hidden, even though a rich man with a geisha mistress is usually keen to show it. However. He'd made his money after the war together with other clever demobilized men. He'd bought up building land. There was a great deal of rebuilding after the bomb damage.

She interrupted, for she could not see why his mother, after caring for him so many years, should relinquish him. As a geisha surely she was a woman with a strong sense of self-respect, so how had she given him up, and why? But she'd gone again with this question into that blank space. His eyes were without depth, screened. Anna turned her head away at the ironies; he was here with her now because of the very forces that were now trying to take him away. Outside, the sound of water falling, marking the current of time. Behind the sound of the water was the deep silence of the mountains. And behind that, the inexorable turning of the earth.

In a sudden sense of loss she cried out, 'Why did you come?'

He misunderstood. 'They tell me to come.'

The rueful laugh, product of a culture that prides itself in its ability to mock the self, shocked him. How could she laugh? Iyyeee . . . he brought his hand up to the back of his head, clutching his hair. A stream of Japanese came out of him.

'If you were sent out of the way, what was that for?'

Now he said nothing.

163

'And why learn English?' she said, more to herself than to him.

He was annoyed. 'I follow business. I have to learn English.'

'He really means you to follow him then.'

'In Japan,' he said slowly, 'we wait for earthquakes. Now not so bad, but before quite terrible.'

She didn't understand.

' . . . They come at any time. You can do nothing but accept and wait.'

With a fury, all her irritation mounted in her. 'Don't accept! Turn your back on them! You've your own life to lead,' she cried, exasperated by his passivity. But she was trotting out the usual western rallying cries more to toughen her own resolve than to strengthen his, and she sensed from the way he held his body that he accepted this attack, even expected it.

The water was flowing continually, drawn from the mountains, making its way to the lake. They had so little time.

'This Oyabun is behind everything. He must have sent Otaki and the others. They use the word "protect". They were sent to watch over you. Did you know?' She couldn't believe he'd always known. Not at first. Surely not, she pleaded.

No, not at first.

She felt exhausted. So . . . he'd probably been told during that telephone call from Hong Kong. Quieter, she went on, 'You're going to have to break away. Whatever they're protecting you from, they're still dictating your life.'

Hideo sat bowed over his knees. She was struggling with resentment. How she wanted him to assert himself; she believed passionately now in the strength of the individual to order his own existence, for hadn't she done just that, in a way? Perhaps she felt that by doing this, by going against the group, he could set himself free. And her too. She could feel his suffering.

He muttered in Japanese. Head down, in English, 'I cannot do it.'

'You *never* question, do you?'

'I cannot.'

(He is a coward, she thought. His life belongs to Oyabun, then.)

The darkness outside stretched away into infinity, taking her question with it. She thought of Okasan, heard her voice, and saw her sitting now, collected, dignified. Would she berate him as Anna had done? Would she plead, hysterically? What of Okasan?

These men manoeuvring contemptuously through an inattentive English suburb. Angrily, she thought they caused less notice to be paid to them than the unusual weather of that winter.

Hideo was withdrawing from her. 'You do not understand us Japanese.'

'Oh, but I do,' pleading, 'I do. At least, I understand you,' putting her hand out and touching him, ' . . . don't I?'

He kept his eyes on her. 'I have to do what is right.'

'Yes,' she insisted eagerly, 'you do.'

'That is to go back. I am not to embarrass my father.'

'Oh dear,' she mocked, the hurt making her voice sarcastically harsh, 'you must not embarrass your father.' But even as the word crossed her lips she felt the imbalance; they did not on the scale of things have the same weight. He meant much more by 'embarrass' – something akin to shame – than she'd given him credit for. He bent his head, staring at the floor.

When he moved, the shock was so sudden she cried out. A torrent of Japanese obliterated everything; he rushed violently past her, with his father's knife he'd snatched up, and ran from the house.

She found herself swaying from side to side, making little whimpering noises. Useless, she was of no use at all any more; she knew nothing of different cultures, different habits of thought, about any other human being – nothing at all. But to act, to try to do something even when the consequences of acting appeared horrific, was second nature to her now. She made the decision the same moment she ran also, out of the house, leaving it open behind her, unattended.

Too dark to see, one could still feel the mass of the mountains. Her feet slap-slapping up the road, as she walked the night creatures closed in around her, and as she concentrated her hearing opened up, mapping the sounds into the far distance. He was following the road, she was sure of it, until it pulled out of the tree-line onto the slates.

Into the cool of the night air, still climbing steadily, made her think in tired fancy that the heat in her was being drawn out by plants with a greedy memory of the hot day. She could smell the pine trees of the higher slopes; ahead the road was lighter, confirming by the inclination of the ground that she was nearly at the top. Again she stopped to listen: wind, the sound of her short panting; and was that the sound of a bark up here on the mountain?

Her footsteps grew slower. Reluctant, and scared. The road was lonely, and it came to her now in what way one lives on levels that are different, simultaneously. And the domestic, everyday level is where we choose to spend our ordinary time, but we're afraid, excited and obsessed at the reminders of those other levels constant to us. Rarely, one can experience all the levels meshed together: it brings an exhilaration of being whole, immersed in life and yet curiously detached. And here at this moment, this was what Anna experienced, even while she became more and more convinced that she wouldn't find the man here, or anywhere. That he was gone; that he'd taken his own strange, predictable way out of his intolerable dilemma. He was torn between duty to his father and his own inclination. Wasn't that the way of it?

She must not go off the road, where the land was treacherous; something ancient in her understood that. She was lightheaded, transformed, and no longer her own person.

166

There was a bark, and a yo yo yo sound echoing round the rocks. Her pace now had such rhythm, the road was as if slipping away beneath her feet, as if the road moved but she did not; so that the shock when she saw his figure suddenly loom towards her was so great she couldn't cry out, only some primitive noise coming from her throat.

Neither of them moved or spoke. There was an immense fatigue growing at finding him there alive, and as she stood quivering, she grew acutely aware of the lower half of her body becoming heavy with lust, animal somehow in the dark, but also it seemed real and natural.

Quite close there was a short, urgent bark; and a rising shriek.

Hideo drove the car. He was silent. And for a time it felt as if they were not leaving but merely going once more to climb the mountains.

Tired, worn from effort, she let her mind drift.

She thought of her husband, feeling differently about him now, and saw as his spirit retreated more from her that her memory of him was softening; he was becoming more like the man she'd fallen in love with, and no longer that displaced self.

She looked over at the hands of the foreigner, relaxed on the steering wheel, a young man's strong slender fingers which had become beloved. Their meeting had changed them both. And she asked herself how she had been changed in a way that had an inevitable quality of destiny. Or so it felt. And yet she'd always believed one made one's own fate; she might have to accept that in some obscure way she'd invited the strange things which had happened to her.

167

She'd been at fault for feeling ordinary people had let her down.

People in general don't ask 'Why me?' when things go well.

She put her head back. They were safe here in the car, and the movement was like the first manoeuvre in the complicated game they were playing to the finish.

After the journey the house was dark and empty. At the back of her mind had been the fear that someone would have got into it while they were away . . . she'd seen it despoiled, broken into. And their own home was no longer sanctuary, although Anna recognized that displacement that results when one has been away, how the rooms lose their familiar proportion, and even the touch of a doorknob feels odd.

It was all so odd. What was going to happen now? She had put barely twenty-four hours between now and the summons from Oyabun: about the time it would take to get back to Japan.

The first casualty in this conflict had been her (revived) sense of humour. To find things amusing, and to feel free to laugh again was freedom; now there didn't seem very much to laugh about at all. And Anna was cross with herself: she'd looked no further than Otaki's skin and teeth, she'd not seen him as a man, and that was a lost opportunity. Now whenever she thought of him she had that maddening memory of him on the television film, forever repeating in her imagination, so that she doubted what she had to remember. How to know about people caused her distress. She'd approached the Japanese rather like an anthropologist, she saw that now, collecting quaintness with delight, making mental lists of oddities in behaviour. But like the difference between

168

the day and night man in Hideo this helped not at all, and explained nothing.

Again that winding walk up the drive of the college. What a crazy building. There was something inappropriate even about its total shape, with turrets, and modern additions and extensions; it was blowsy, over-decorated like a hopeless old pro. Here as well was that same unoccupied quiet Anna found in her road, still so many people away or houses vacant. The heatwave had dried up the plants, adding to the air of neglect, bringing a premature drop of leaves which were swirling dustily at the foot of the steps. Walking down the tiled and cool corridor Anna saw that everything had been cleared away; the notice boards empty of all but one programme for the autumn.

Anna looked greatly improved, Clare thought. She was sorting books in the main part of the library. 'Why did you come back so soon? Nearly everyone's away here. Just one caretaker. Something obviously caused a change of plan; the summer students are either in central London or gone abroad. Probably some crisis over money. But I haven't been told to go yet, so . . .'

Anna was tongue-tied before Clare. What could it be: shame, fright, fear of ridicule?

Clare would soon be going away herself, and a reluctance to see anyone else made Anna ask what particular divide she'd crossed when she'd left with Hideo. A teasing remark about Hideo's habits made her realize that she'd ceased to notice them. Who had changed, he or she; or had they both adapted?

But outside the house she looked about with a sinking heart; the emptiness of a town is unnerving in a way the countryside can never be. The house where David and Janet had lived had been so gone over and treated that it had become truly anonymous, and no trace of the occupants, no sign of their tastes, remained. Even the exuberant wildness of their front garden, more the result of neglect than deliberate policy, had been tamed and reduced to the correct manner for attracting the right kind of tenant.

Anna felt no guilt, but photographs of Gregory on a table were forlorn nevertheless, and she was impelled to ask Fay to put flowers there. As she went about catching up with household tasks she asked what the future might hold. She did not get far. Never as far as imagining herself leaving for another country; the real obsession was what might happen tomorrow, or next week.

'Everyone's away still. What shall we do?' A child's complaint.

Underneath their bare feet were the blackened cherry stones still with stalks.

'Very dry. The garden is spoiled,' Hideo was saying. He had not recovered his spirits since leaving the Lakes. He stayed in his room.

'It'll be fine if we water,' Anna said brightly; but he shook his head, 'I think not,' looking upwards into the tree where Anna saw the tips of leaves turning pink already. One or two leaves falling.

'It's just the heat.'

After the children had gone upstairs they sat uneasily. They both said they were tired. But he looked well, his skin like hers was brown, his black hair glossy. It had grown. Turning out the lights, Anna at the window could feel Hideo's arm as it came round her only a few evenings ago. And the emptiness of the space around her now was unbearable. What was the wise thing to do? In a ferment of indecision she fumed: was she to be ruled by her emotions? Could she not use her head? And what the hell did it matter any longer, either way?

She was locking up, turning out lights, checking, back in her role as guardian. At the hall she stopped for the letters. She was sure there'd be no newspaper cuttings, but there was one new development in the form of a polite note. A Mr Misumi had information for her. An invitation to take tea with him and his wife at an address in Holland Park. So, it appeared that Anna was not finished with hearing from strange Japanese gentlemen. She felt colder, and crept into her bed.

Hideo didn't know the name. Anna noticed, sadly, how uncommunicative he was, as if his temperament changed more with geography than circumstance, and to all her questions and suppositions it was his usual phrases of 'maybe' or 'it is possible', until in irritation she stated he didn't know and clearly didn't care. At this he blushed, like a youth, apologizing.

As she took the underground to a part of London she'd never visited before, Anna reflected on the alteration in her view of places. She inhabited different worlds since she'd known Hideo, and although she knew she moved in her own country she was detached from it, observing somewhat from the side like a traveller in an unfamiliar land. It was a loss of some sort. It was certainly unsettling to find that the address should turn out to be uncomfortably near an overpass, with the blare of traffic roaring and a sight of the cars level with the upper windows. It was an unfortunate choice for Mr Misumi.

She'd tried not to have any preconceived ideas, but had not thought to meet an elderly man with a face of old ivory. She'd been let in by a round bowing woman muttering expressions of welcome, a fact made incongrous by her wearing western dress.

Mr Misumi, however, was dressed in a sombre dark blue yukata, and their house was like them, a mixture of the western and oriental. Beckoning Anna to a chair, he sat opposite, his wife preferring to kneel.

171

'*Do itashi mashite* is what we say: you are welcome.' Mrs Misumi nodded and added some remark. 'She understands,' he said, 'but she is too stupid to speak any words.' Mrs Misumi gave a little nod of acquiescence.

Directly in front of Anna was a low table, and arranged with care some recognizable sweets.

'*Dozo.*' Mrs Misumi proferred them, but Anna refused. Mr Misumi made elegant comments about the weather and Anna's children, sufficient for her to find out his knowledge of her affairs, and his command of English.

They might then have sat forever in silence but Anna was too impatient. 'Who gave you my name, Mr Misumi?' praying it was not Professor Otaki.

'The mother of Hideo Ishida. She is concerned about his welfare. He is now *yoshi.*'

'*Yoshi?*'

'Adopted son. She did not want you to have any misunderstandings about the situation.'

'What situation?'

Again there was such a pause that Anna went through the possibilities of apologizing, or asking the question again in different words, or changing the subject in the hope they'd get back to the important business by a roundabout route. Mr Misumi was, however, a patient man, explaining his position in England, where he was working on an academic project to do with Buddhism. Mrs Misumi listened to her husband, giving little nods as he listed the various sects and the differences between them that made his study essential.

Anna's patience had been tested. 'I don't know much about that,' she said, somewhat artlessly.

'Do you know *anything* about Japan?' his question sharp as a knife.

Taken aback. Well, there'd been these programmes; she'd read books . . . Mrs Misumi gasped at the mention of Sei Shonagon.

Mr Misumi smiled. Like a beatific Buddha.

172

Anna found herself apologizing: she knew that was a long time ago . . .

'The Japanese are a conventional people. It does not seem long to us.' This certainly sounded like a snub.

He smoothed his kimono. As if this was a signal, his wife made noises and went off, as her husband explained, to prepare some tea. While Anna wondered if they would make a ceremony of it, Mr Misumi settled his hands squarely on his knees. 'You know, of course, that we Japanese like most to live in harmony?'

One knew that, of course.

'It is, I think, to an extent true, that you have not been wholly successful in aiding your young guest to achieve this.'

Anna's indignation kept her mute.

'Most unfortunate.'

Anna held her tongue.

'I have, I think, to inform you of some aspects of Hideo Ishida which you will, of course, not know.'

What had he done? Anna began to put together a picture from the soft brushstrokes of Mr Misumi's language, of a young Hideo who after being adopted had been sent away for some breach of etiquette, or some misdemeanour, or (such was the gravity on the man's face opposite) some real disgrace. What could it have been? There he was, at a private university, so what had he done? Joined the Communist Party perhaps, or worse, the Red Brigade (and Anna remembered hearing of the brutal executions meted out to their own members some years previously). But Mr Misumi was explaining that once the young man has gone through the hell of the entrance exams he is more or less left to run a bit – as it were – wild: to sow his 'wild oats' (this Mr Misumi produced from his considerable repertoire). So, had Hideo got some young lady pregnant, and caused scandal? Had he tried to procure an abortion? Had he gone around getting drunk and abusing members of Parliament?

He had been too independent.

What?

Mrs Misumi entered. With English tea. In her confusion, Anna commented (she was trying to be gracious): What beautiful cups! Were they Victorian? Were they antique?

Mrs Misumi, when she finally understood, was shocked. Oh no. She didn't like old things. She dabbed her mouth with her little napkin.

So Anna's sin was that she had encouraged Hideo to be independent?

We have a saying, put in Mr Misumi: the nail that sticks out gets hit back in.

She never knew whether to laugh or get mad. This could not be the reason behind the newspaper cuttings, or who sent them. Anna stared at the sweets. She realized they had some way to go in explanations.

From where she was sitting the sight of the car wheels rushing repeatedly past was becoming hypnotic, and added to her sense of a relentless pressing-down of doom. What was Mr Misumi's interest in Hideo? Had the mother requested he help?

But Mr Misumi, with no trace of embarrassment, said that he'd known her intimately when she was a geisha, before she came under the care of her other patron.

Mr Ishida? Ah no, for hadn't Hideo said all was finished now between them? There was, as she was finding out in other directions, something missing.

'The goal for all Japanese is their good name. They do not want in any way to be conspicuous; they want to belong;' and Hideo, he went on, would not be able to bear his mother's reproaches.

But whether he wanted to go or stay, he was still a grown man, couldn't he be allowed to make up his own mind?

To avoid detraction one has to give up personal gratification. This was stated firmly. It is the Japanese way. In the past, loss of face was an evil worse than death itself, hence one could only redeem one's honour through honourable suicide. Loss of the face.

Anna thought back over her reactions to Hideo, at first thinking him childish and ill-educated, next in need of protecting; as she knew him better, in need of being loved.

'We Japanese learn very fast, and from the West,' Mr Misumi was continuing over Anna's thoughts. 'We do not want our young people to be corrupted; we are not happy with too much individualism – '

'He was never left to live his own life,' Anna protested, aware that somehow one was going from point a to b but that at any moment one could jump to m and not know how one got there. 'His mother was always ringing him up.'

'What else was she to do?' His voice was unexpectedly sharp. Mrs Misumi reacted, but only by bending her head.

Anna shifted uncomfortably. 'I believe,' she stated, from conviction, 'that there was always more to this than a mother's concern.'

Mrs Misumi sweetly offered more tea, and when Anna refused, gathered up the cups with mannered calm and left the room. At what point was it right to get up and leave? An instinctive English notion of when a visit is at an end was no good here. Nothing concrete had been said. With deliberation she studied the face of Mr Misumi. It was remarkable in being flat like a dish. When he turned to his wife Anna could see that he had hooded eyes like a chameleon, with the bulge of the eyeball projecting beyond the frontal bone; she found this odd, and slightly repellent. Hideo was a good-looking man, his face symmetrical, and somehow twentieth-century acceptable. Mr Misumi had a physiognomy which underlined for Anna the old difference between the European and the Oriental, for he was a man whose face belonged with the woodblock and the ivory. She tried to think of this man as the ardent admirer of Hideo's mother as geisha, and failed.

'Was his mother angry because he took some holiday with me?' She blushed.

'He is a young man a long way from his country; it does not

175

matter what he does.' Again he'd not replied as she expected. He added, 'He has no responsibilities away from home.'

'No. And he's had freedom here. He's been able to be himself.'

'I think you are mistaken perhaps.' Mr Misumi smiled gently. 'To be cut off from home is a terrible thing for us.'

Why was it that every time they had an exchange something seemed to slip?

With Mrs Misumi out of the room Anna dared ask more searching questions and, thinking back to the close, loving life of the young child – how he shares the mother's bed, the breast-fed dependency – she wanted to ask whether Hideo could be seen as resenting his father, of wanting to disobey? It was such a struggle for a Westerner to think into these minds from the other side of the world, people without their Christian ethic, without their Freud, their guilt. But how to put this?

Mr Misumi had been in England long? He sighed: some years. He made it seem like exile. Why then hadn't . . . what was the mother's name . . . ?

Shima-San. A gentle name. It did not help with the enigma of Okasan.

. . . Why hadn't he been asked to help instead of Professor Otaki? A great deal might have been avoided if Otaki had never been involved.

'Ahhh . . . Professor Otaki is Mr Ishida's man.' He sucked in his breath. There was a long pause. 'Mr Ishida seems to have everything his own way.' After all Hideo had done what was asked of him. He'd learnt, his intentions were good . . .

'That is no alibi for failure. One cannot change the rules in Japan.'

Failure? Mr Misumi had rapped out that last remark as if it was an immutable law laid down by the gods. What conceivable failure? A soft tap on the door was bringing Mrs Misumi bearing another tray, and beckoning Anna in front of the low table, she and her husband knelt on cushions at either side,

176

leaving Anna with an absurd sense of being a ticking clock between two ornamental cats.

'*Dozo.*' It was a black laquered tray; there were little delicacies, fortunately a still life, of shrimps and raw fish.

'*Arigato.*' The tea, frog green, and frothy, tasted a little bitter, and good.

Mrs Misumi clapped her hands. '*Do itashi mashite.*'

Having scored her point, Anna felt she could go on. Anything to force the revelations that were so badly needed. 'I am *gaijin*,' she said, 'so perhaps the mother of Hideo does not like me.'

'She is afraid for her son.' On the excuse of dealing with the dishes Mrs Misumi again left the room. Then he began to talk; but as if all that had been said before had been so much idle chatter. 'We depend', he said, 'on international trade. We have to trade to survive. This is vitally important for us. We had bad time over oil some years ago, and that made some people think about after the war years when things were so very hard.' He paused and added that Kuneo Ishida was forty years older than his son, and he remembered.

In her mind Anna saw the film running again, and heard the commentary repeating in her head. She pushed it away.

'So Hideo has to go back to do what he doesn't want: work in his father's business.'

'Economic achievement is a noble thing. If he has will-power he will succeed.'

'But this is big business, and that is a different thing. And what of this "failure" in him, his being "independent"?'

Mr Misumi had brought his fingertips together and was pressing them. 'He is a little unpractised, perhaps, in this international market, this kind, but there will be others to help him to succeed.'

Anna looked down at her hands. Success for her meant now a satisfying relationship, a life that had some significance, or to be of help to others. But success for Hideo was to lie not in love, not in individual freedom, but in being Japanese. She lifted a piece of raw fish, and biting into it found the flesh lingering softly on her tongue, unexpectedly difficult for her teeth; a strange business, this rawness to someone used to the cooked. Outside she was aware of the noise of the passing traffic.

Mr Misumi sighed. 'Shima feels that her son must not betray tradition. She is not free to consult her feelings. She also must bow to the inevitable.' He stopped, waiting for this opaque remark to touch her. 'There is also the question of the mother of Kuneo Ishida.'

Anna leant forward. What was to come now?

'Perhaps you do not know . . . children in Japan represent husband's family-line, so, in tradition, the mother-in-law has greater claim on them even than the wife. She feels her intentions must be consulted.'

'Even when he is adopted?' Anna reflected that some property might be involved, and this might account for such a ridiculous and outmoded meddling. Mrs Misumi gave signs of finding Anna's tone too brusque, for her hand lifted and fluttered in front of her mouth, and she said something aside to her husband.

'She is saying to you that they have a fear of losing Japanese quality.' He was translating, while Mrs Misumi continued under her breath words which were impossible for Anna to understand, although there appeared a ghost of something she recognized. And Mr Misumi turned in irritation, it seemed, crossly saying 'MacDonald', and then 'Beatles', as if correcting pronunciation, and Anna found it suddenly immensely difficult not to laugh aloud. For if these were the influences that petrified old Japanese grandmothers . . .

'You must realize we cannot do what we want. We cannot have separate allegiances. It is not possible for us.'

Getting to her feet . . . Anna knew little more than continuing obscurities. All hints, nothing definite, yet she sensed that Mr Misumi, in some way exiled from his country, had tried in an oblique way to indicate danger, anxiety, complication. He'd made the insubstantial figure of Hideo's mother become more woman; he'd known her as Hideo could not. A small dejected smile had formed on Anna's mouth. This was it. She had been 'informed'. They were by the front door, and Anna was slipping off the house shoes when she thought to ask about Japanese foxes.

'Fox!' Mr Misumi had jerked upright from surprise, then he laughed, rather too long Anna decided, as if he had been holding himself in. Foxes are changeable, moving from animal to human or from human to animal, and no one knowing which.

'Not all bad then?'

'No, no. There were some fine women who were foxes and cherished their children, and some men . . .'

'All old stories, of course.'

'Old stories, but people still clap hands at Inari shrine. You know Inari is God of prosperous business?'

Anna burst out laughing. He would be, of course.

'His messengers are foxes.' Plainly Mr Misumi was puzzled.

Anna had her coat on, and one finger ready on the catch of her umbrella, waiting, as husband and wife were deciding something soberly together. They had something to show her. So. She sought the truth, and she'd asked about foxes. His wife padded away and almost immediately came back with a largish box made from a red wood. A benign-looking face showed between the doors of the box – a portable shrine maybe – and as he held it out, Anna took it, curious to see. O Inari Sama was seated astride a fox in some comfort. The fox, though, was not, for it was twisted round and was looking up at the deity with a half-grin, half-snarl, and reversing it Anna saw why, or rather did not see at all: for the fox had its legs bent round the wrong way and most disturbingly was displaying a large erect phallus. What was this? Inari's, or the fox's little joke? The more she stared, the worse it became. Misumi man and wife regarded her with no trace of embarrassment on their side. Anna found she had to clear her

179

throat. This was quite old, no doubt? Yes indeed. Anna considered the front view again where it appeared that Inari had his messenger where he wanted him. The message one could read from the back was different. If one was laundering dirty money, she was thinking, like Kuneo Ishida, then all that needed to be put right from the spiritual side was to clap hands for Inari, put in a coin, ring the bell, bow the head and all was done. But the fox, though, who carried the messages, was a bit untrustworthy perhaps? Anna handed the box back. How interesting! She wished the Japanese with their known passion for order would tidy up their mythology. She didn't dare to ask whether this particular fox could change his shape. Mr Misumi had too literal a mind.

Her own road had the tired and dusty look of high summer; the leaves of the privet showed a coating of sticky black. The road itself, though, suburban and laid out, had that comfortable air of the undisturbed middle classes. Anna had supposed she belonged here at least. Now she no longer did; she didn't know where her place was. Or who her own people were.

Hideo did not want to hear about Mr Misumi. He was agitated and pale, yet excited. Anna had never seen him so distracted. But look, she insisted, he must pay attention; Mr Misumi had a message from his mother.

'Ho! Aiee!' He hit his head in perplexity. 'It was my father who rang. And he wants to talk with you.'

Anna started laughing. It began to be silly.

'Don't laugh!' He was deadly serious. Anna sobered. Kuneo had not long hung up. He had rung — therefore in what was to him the night.

She asked how Hideo could stand such interference?

'It's lonely deciding for yourself.' He appeared to be in a sulk.

The adult person has to, in her society at any rate; why so peevish? But this was not their way of it. One consulted family and friends, one had a conference, and then one made a decision that was by some process agreed on by everybody. These mysterious shifts and adjustments, though fascinating, in the end appalled her. Anna tried again to say what Mr Misumi had conveyed, but on hearing his mother's name Hideo started. He sounded displeased. 'Her name is Miyako!'

In her mind's eye the woman who did ikebana was floating away, washed out by brushstrokes.

'Mr Misumi calls her Shima,' she said quietly for he'd spoken so abruptly. 'He was close to her.'

'Geisha name.' He spoke dismissively, giving her a quick look, rather chilling, and she had again this perturbed sense that he was being bent away from her, by what agency she couldn't know. So she went out into the garden, which she'd seen since her return as surrounded by the urban jungle, the human wild. For Hideo the city spoke reassurance; for her this was no longer true. The setting sun was making a yellow and apricot sky, and in the cherry tree two pigeons were greedily ripping what remained of the fruit. Kuneo Ishida still had not rung. What was his motive in ringing in the middle of his night? Slipping her feet out of her shoes to cool them on the grass, she put her hand out to touch the smooth shining trunk. Spring returns to trees. Hideo came behind her, and without turning to him she said, 'I think I love you.'

'I too feel love for you. It is good in your garden, Anna-San.'

'Sometimes.'

It was dusk soon, and the last of the swifts were still chasing insects as the first of the bats came hunting. There were no barriers for them. They went in, and shut the doors

181

with reluctance. Throughout the evening both of them would pass the telephone. But it didn't ring that night.

When the telephone rang the next day, she jumped as if scalded.

The voice was as she remembered it: breathless and slightly hoarse, the voice of one who had heart problems, maybe. He was talking slowly in English phrases, with pauses between as if he was reading from a script or prepared remarks. The pronunciation also was bad; she had to concentrate hard to get the sense.

The first phrases she hardly paid attention to anyway (as they were merely politeness) for she was hearing behind the words the tone of one used to command, faintly weary as if going through a necessary chore, and when he spoke of whether she had enough money Anna saw red, took the opportunity, and interrupted. Hideo had said his father knew everything; well, she wanted him to explain.

There was the same breathy pause. 'It is not our way to explain ourselves.'

'Forgive me, it is our way to expect explanations.'

Again the long pause. Was he sitting alone in his Tokyo office, was there someone with him listening in?

'Ahhh . . . I want my son to be professional man. We are very big organization and we do much business all over the world now.' The voice rasped on while Anna barely held in her impatience; none of her questions were going to be answered. But what she was being told was meant to impress, with its descriptions of associations growing round the world, of bank accounts and the movements of currency, of shipping interests, building concerns, light industries . . . It was clear he had entrepreneurial flair, he was a highly successful man, but nevertheless . . . He stopped. 'Such interests have problems. I had many problems. People try to injure me,'

She was not going to help him by asking any more.

'Mrs Dean. You listen! To enrich oneself is natural. So no weakness in my organization. We successful. We make money, and we have power, that is the way we learn from the Americans in the last war. Have targets. Have goals. Have projects. It is good idea, I think. It works. Have you been paid enough money, Mrs Dean?'

In angry astonishment she lost her power to answer; she felt she might break down.

'Money is important thing, Mrs Dean. You have children. We find you have no husband . . .' As he became more agitated, the careful phrases started to collapse. ' . . . They tell various distortions. Business is troublesome. It demand loyalty. I think you make harsh criticism.'

Anna gave a derisive laugh. It no longer amused her that he put *r*s in place of his *l*s. 'Keep your money!'

He began to chuckle, immediately followed by a fit of harsh coughing, coming down the wires to hit her eardrums. She repeated: keep the money.

'So . . . English. You have it now. I tell them to do all.'

'And they do, because they're scared stiff of you.'

He gave a fruity laugh, as though complimented. 'Everyone scare Mr Chairman;' and as if this finished everything conveniently, 'Tell Hideo I leave here tomorrow.'

Where was here?

'Zurich.'

So the previous day when they had imagined him ringing in the night from Tokyo . . .? Again this amused him. No, he'd rung from London that time. He'd seen to things.

During all this talk he'd never once mentioned the woman Miyako. Anna's sympathies had widened, for as she'd found out more about her, so the far-off woman – anxious, proud, one of an esoteric breed – had lost the aspect of mother,

183

professional woman, to that of victim. Victims lose the sense
of who and what they are. So to whom was she now Miyako?

'Hideo?' Familiar and yet become foreign again for her
since this talk with his father, Anna was tugged by conflicting emotions. She asked why it was she had such a strong
impression of coldness as well as intelligence in his querying
look? How could their closeness be cancelled out? She pointed
out that crucial facts had been withheld from them both and
watched his response. Ishida's deceit freed her from any guilt:
she owed him nothing, and had obligations only to Hideo.
The face is the individual, she wanted to say; why otherwise
do you hide behind the polite face, the mask. It's what you
are yourself that's important; it's what you make of your life,
not what others make for you that is of value. All this she
wanted to say, but she didn't think she'd chiselled at the
words well enough for him to follow.

Along the airport barrier, waiting, Anna and the children
were between two groups of Indians.

They had arrived early to see this pageant of Indians
embracing and shouting while their women stood back,
holding onto children and bags, before drifting away. Flights
from Montreal, from Abu Dhabi, from Osaka, and from the
Bahamas where her parents had been. Then places to the left
had been taken by Arabs, white-robed for the most part, their
feet in western shoes, incurious, slightly contemptuous at the
company perhaps; they talked softly together. Backpackers
with reddened knees came through smartly, joking. Where
from? One couldn't read the labels. All these people with
their cultural patterns, their preconceptions, prejudice and
blind-spots, swirling around like different shoals of fish. Anna

vas bumped on her other side; she smiled into the slant eyes
when their mother gently admonished them. They were
noticeably quieter than Nick, who had just kicked the barrier
and sent a shock-wave through the metal into the elbow of one
of the Arabs.

People who, to guess from their angry tans, had been
recently in the Caribbean started coming through, and then to
her delight Anna saw her father had got himself behind the
Japanese, and towering above them gave the impression of
trying to wade carefully through, a shepherd surrounded by his
sheep.

But again, like a blow on the head, Anna felt herself knocked
from her centre seeing her parents seeking her out, their smiles
of welcome. She had expected everything to anchor back
securely; she'd been waiting for it. But it didn't happen. As
they drew nearer, smiles ever wider, her heart sank from
disappointment.

Back at the house, Hideo was not there, as Anna had
suspected.

'Wily young man. He's not frightened of us, surely?'

'I'm glad you made use of the car, Anna,' her father was
saying as they walked about the garden. He started to pluck at
weeds as a preliminary to asking whether anything had
happened. He was always the spokesman for the two of them.

'What could have happened?'

'I'm not a fool. And I don't want to pry but . . . I mean
between you and this young Japanese.' He cleared his throat.
'One can tell the difference in you, if one is close, of course.' He
pulled more weeds while Anna silently stood by him, and as he
dropped them into the compost, dusting off his hands, she saw,
so heightened with tension as she was, his hands were now
stained with green. 'It would not be suitable.'

'Suitable!'

'Please don't get me wrong. Ah you have, I can see. Forgive
me. But think carefully. I mean – '

Her voice came out flat, as if uninvolved. 'He has to go back.'

185

'He has? So we might not ever meet. A pity. A great pity, in many ways.'

They did not say anything about having the children to stay.

Nick asked as they waved the grandparents and the car away, couldn't a car be bought with all that money?

They only just made ends meet as it was.

'Ask for more. Hideo'll give it you.' He smiled seductively. 'Then we could get away from here. I hate this place.'

'It's your home.'

'Everything's different.' His little-boy look had come on his face. He felt, like her she was sure, the former life closing in again around them, but then as children will, more resilient than their adults, he shrugged and dismissed the problem. It would sort itself out.

That night Anna found it very hard to get to sleep. Hideo had not returned home. She'd forced herself to stay awake, and then, tired out, tossed with insomnia. And slept only to dream of standing outside a long low house, where a woman was telling her to go in and stop thinking about foxes. It was a place of sliding doors, but to open them she had to get on her knees and slide from a small hole in their base. Each time the doors stuck, and when released slid to show another room beyond, more doors, and each room got progressively darker until she was feeling her way blindly, fingers outstretched. She awoke to find herself gripping the sheet, and instinctively turned to the bedroom door. Hideo stood there. She did not move.

'Anna?'

She did not reply. And he didn't ask a second time.

It was raining, a persistent drizzle. London was full of damp tourists, in twos and threes, moving slowly. Most of them had provided themselves (such is the reputation of England) with devices for keeping off the rain. Catching someone's curious look, Anna realized suddenly how she was being experienced as a native by them. She'd gone racing late in the afternoon down to the bank to check the state of her account. The sum she saw recorded so took her breath away that she inserted the card three times. She ran home, a foxy grin swimming in the rain before her face.

'Why are you sitting in the darkness?'

'I am thinking.'

She asked if she could put on the light. 'Just a small light if you like.'

'It is your house.'

'Well . . . if you prefer to sit in the dark. What's the matter?' She got down before the couch where he sat, slackly, his energy gone. Choosing her words with care: 'Do you feel you have to go back?'

He thought before answering. 'I know I have to go back, but what I feel . . . '

Anna said slowly, 'I know I want you to stay.'

'I think Okasan does not want me to come back. Not now. She finds something out, I think.' He sighed. In the dim light his eyes were total black. She let her gaze linger; he was pushing the hair away from his face. Okasan would see the change in him. He had fined out, the young soft look had been replaced by taut skin over the cheekbones.

'You will come to see me? You will come to Japan?'

So, he had decided. Of course, she said, sarcastic from hurt, she would come to see the cherry blossom.

His face brightened. 'That is good idea. Bery good idea.' Why was his accent deteriorating? She couldn't speak.

A small frown making a crease vertical between his brows, he looked doubtfully at her. 'You do not mean what you say, do you?'

'No. I was being sarcastic . . . ironic, if you like.'

'Like? I like? You are hard to understand.'

'It's the English way. It helps us when we are feeling bitter.'

'Better? How feeling better?'

'Bitter! Resentful. Angry.'

'Ah . . . you feel bitter. My fault?'

'Would a Japanese woman say yes?'

'I think so. And she would hit me.'

Anna, melting at this blunt acceptance of hurt and retaliation: 'I don't want to hit you.'

'You are not Japanese. She would hit,' he said with pride, as if the hitting demonstrated the force of the feeling provoked.

'It is not my fault I am not Japanese.'

'Anna-San, please.'

'How can I *possibly* come and see you in Japan?'

'I will pay. No problem.' Eager suddenly like a boy. She felt her face crumple, and turned swiftly away from him.

'What of America?' She knew she should not talk of it. His face coloured, and he untwisted his legs and stood up. 'There will be nothing for yourself if you go back. You will belong to him. And the organization.'

'I have to go for my father. I owe my father.'

'I hate your father.'

He didn't seem to mind this, merely raising his eyebrows in a new gesture. Outside, the dense dark of a wet night.

Looking into the darkness Anna could hear again the lecturing voice of Mr Misumi: 'You cannot understand Mr Ishida. He is much admired top man. He is a bit gangster, like Mishima, but we do not mind that. He is top man but he is secret man. You know bunraku puppets . . . ?' and Anna had nodded, warily. 'Bunraku have operators who move eyes, turn heads, open and shut mouths of puppets so that they appear quite alive. Operators dress in black, like shadows. Now listen. Kuneo Ishida makes himself into shadow, and people know about him, but do not know him.'

She said aloud, 'Your father is involved with Yakuza. He is Oyabun,' stating this as if it were her trump card, but he merely looked surprised at her naïvety. Of course they do

188

dirty business but, he went on eagerly, they never involve ordinary people.

He'd spoken with the measured calm of absolute certainty. In the same tone Mr Misumi had said Yakuza have their place. Dark place. 'They deal with business where police would rather not go. You have a saying: Get a thief to catch a thief.' And he'd lifted his tea in a gesture Anna saw was habitual and polished from long practice, making the movement smooth from beginning to end, his elbow bending outwards as he brought the cup to his mouth. It seemed to admit no other way of drinking tea.

'But they *do*! They *do* involve ordinary people. Your father has put money into my bank. A great deal of it!'

'That is good,' His face lighting up with a broad smile. 'Now you can come to Japan.'

But trying to make him see how his father had been moving money and assets, even people round the world, he shrugged: a politician needs funds. 'You want to give back? Very peculiar, Anna, I do not understand.'

'It's bribery, you know.'

'No. It is thanks.'

'It can't be. And I shall give it back.'

He looked annoyed, a flush on his face. 'Why? He shows you much honour. Yes. You cannot do this. It will be . . . ' and he searched for the right word, ' . . . a very harsh thing.'

Outside, the rain had increased, and large drops rolling together down the window-pane caught the light from the lamp and were turned to silver. A shiver passed through her. The house hung uneasily round her like a garment gone misshapen. She whispered: what had become of the knife? Not knowing why she had to ask.

He walked over and stood very close behind her as if the question had taken away anger, but they did not touch. She could feel the heat from his body. 'I was going to bury it but . . . Oh, anyway . . . ' he said.

*

'Otaki and his side-kick.' It was the short, thick-set one they apparently called Honda. Their presence at her house she had to accept, like the weather, but Anna would not lift a finger more or let them inside until Hideo agreed. Thank God the children were out with friends.

His eyes widened, 'Hor . . . here?' and then narrowed, but he came down from his room. Closely watching them in the hall for that precise angle of bow, she saw only hasty movements which in no way defined the status of each other. Honda almost immediately leant himself against the wall. His suit had a greasy look and he was surveying her house with what looked like contempt. Otaki had not wasted his time but was giving what seemed to be a series of orders, for Hideo ran upstairs for papers.

Otaki turned his penetrating eyes onto her. 'You received the money, Mrs Dean?'

How he loved to be on top.

'It is in the bank.' To keep it means being corrupted and no Shinto ceremony would wash it off her hands. 'But if I can find a way to give it back – '

'Ha! What did you expect? Mr Ishida has been generous.'

She couldn't stand the superior smile. He was studying her in silence, lit that customary cigarette and continued smoking. She wouldn't even offer him an ashtray. Several things were clear: she had been used, as a convenience, and it was lowering to see herself as just another foreign woman, useful for this and that. Unimportant. Briefly a nuisance, but not a big nuisance. A boredom came off both men. His training, she noticed, forbade him to drop ash even on her floor.

'What did you expect, Mrs Dean? Gratitude? This was the

190

arrangement. You cooked. You gave him tea . . . ' he sniggered, ' . . . even with sugar. You had nice young man who treats you as Mama-San. Very good. And you are an education to him . . . '

Hideo was coming slowly down the stairs.

'And I tell Mr Ishida that you kidnap his son so he is very kind to give so much money. He forgives.'

Masculine dominance she knew about, misery she knew about, survival she was learning, so she swallowed. Her anger had settled at the base of her throat and kept her without words.

'*Asobi*. You know that word? You ask about words, I think. It is what the young men do when they are taken away from Okasan. His father expects him to play. *He*, Ishida-San?' and he rattled off in Japanese. Honda let out a guffaw and eased his trousers with his thumbs inside the waistband in a gesture that was obscene and obscurely menacing. Hideo, still on the stairs in that stained-glass light, was pale, but he neither looked at her, nor spoke.

'Have you no shame?' Her head was aching now, the pulse heavy and throbbing.

Otaki seemed amused. 'Shame? We leave that at home.'

The telephone began to ring. In the hall all four had ears turned to the sound as if expecting a summons. With her stomach churning, Anna went to be by herself in her room.

But it was Louise from America. Her voice, normally exuberant, now estatic, laughing: she had got married again. Wasn't that crazy! She was so happy. Had to share it. Dear Anna, dearest Anna, all your fault, of course.

'My fault? How?'

'Oh, I don't know. Anna, he's so beautiful. I'd forgotten how absolutely . . . ' Her voice went on and on. Anna, interjecting a word when she could to show she was still on the line, began to get a chilling sense of how it was her fault. Her air of loneliness had preyed upon Louise, that was probably it.

191

'You said you'd never marry again.'

'Well, one changes. I changed my mind.'

They would stay in California for a bit . . . the weather so lovely . . . Anna should really come . . .

Anna went down in a murderous mood. Hideo had his eyes on her; she knew she was experiencing a dangerous anger. Could he ask Mr Honda if he or the other man had ever sent any presents here? Or letters?

Hideo's questions in his own language sounded terse. Hoh, Honda asked pointing at himself. Eh?

Uhh, Otaki said, his manner abrupt, the words few.

Hai. Honda agreed to something, with reluctance. But nothing more was said.

They left and Hideo went back to his room without a backward glance, leaving Anna alone. The open front door had let in the damp air, caught unwarmed by the sun round that north-east front of the house; it hung around with the cigarette smoke, and the hall now chilled her to the bone.

It was restless weather. Some days fine beginning and then becoming quickly overcast and squally, bringing yet more heavy rain. The barometer rose and fell. The gusts of wind had done final damage to the fence, and a fox, should there be a fox, could walk through with ease. The leaves with the dry autumn had been rich, a red and a brown-spotted yellow; caught near the broken fence in piles they were fading in the wet to a nondescript colour. Moving back towards the house after looking at this damage, Anna saw just the white tips of the children's fingers making patterns on the misted window-panes; from here these signs looked like hopeless kanji to Susanoo, a spoilt brat of a god, in charge of storms. The disconsolate children irritated her so much that she went against her scruples, walking them to the local cinema and leaving them there to see cartoons and eat sweets.

She was waiting. There was nothing she could do.

Hideo was out again. Always out. Living on the edge of his nerves, she felt, and having to avoid her. She kept on asking what he was going to do. What was going to happen? She found her mind drawn back to the television films, the books, the talk of arranged marriage, and it made her laugh, but most uncomfortably, to think how she'd fallen for the exotic, how she'd lost herself among all the data and the chaos of information. She'd been most willingly seduced.

She went up to his vacant room as if trespassing, hesitating at the door. Though the room was, as usual, straight, he gave no signs of doing any work any more. The only thing was the neat, black Japanese notebook. She looked at the fine and organized script. Opening the book had done her no good; he had, she thought with resentment, penetrated her secrets. He had taken from her but given back not enough, nowhere near enough. The face in the mirror she was polishing sent back puzzlement and a wariness, but the pain inside appeared not to show, and she saw now, with her eyes travelling round the outline, that her face had also become finer, the fleshy flab left after Gregory's death having disappeared, and the eyes gravely regarding the image seemed to reflect back and forth, receding further and further inwards. Her hand reached firmly out, wiping across the image with a cloth.

It was all so quiet. Since the return, only a great silence came from Japan, and the telephone hardly rang. At the sound of the doorbell she gave a start, although she'd been expecting a summons, and from her side of the door heard feet retreating back down the steps as if not wanting directly to confront her.

The short rectangle of Mr Misumi stood dripping, looking upwards at Anna as she looked down the steps at him.

193

'Hideo is not in.'

'I regret.' He dealt efficiently with his umbrella, took off his shoes, apologizing for his socks; refusing the comfortable blue chair he sat, and for a few minutes composed himself. In this bad light from the rain he still showed himself worn and tired.

'Shima is dead. She took her life.'

So something had broken at long last in Miyako. One cannot ask why, one cannot ask how. With an inevitability, it now appeared, the story on the other side of the world had run its course, and she who had gone through so many disguises had made her last shape-shift.

'She has gone to Buddha.'

Mr Misumi refused tea. He sat pensively for more minutes while Anna's mind became a turmoil of pity and curiosity and dread.

Anna said, 'I am so sorry. What made her do it?'

Mr Misumi's hooded eyelids hid any expression. His voice was neutral. He sighed. 'I do not know. Maybe she felt too much shame. It is the mother's fault if the child errs.'

Oh . . . Anna turned her head away. How could Hideo have erred? She thought her son will not come back maybe?

He considered this, and repeated he did not know.

'Excuse me, so sorry, but I tell you private things . . . Shima was in impossible situation. She broke promise.'

Anna waited, pulse heavy in her throat.

'She promised to give up son. Not to telephone. Not to do anything. You understand? She makes over son to father. He says she has house, she will get money so no problems that way, but only if she leaves Hideo alone. Never to contact. If she contacts all money goes; her son goes.'

'But she couldn't do that!'

'Yes. She is not strong enough not to want to know about her son.'

'It is too cruel. Why should he make her do such a thing?'

'Ahhh . . . Shima was always tender, but strong. She had

194

what we call *yugen*, something mysterious, very proud. She came from samurai, from Oshima, the old world. But Kuneo Ishida is what you call self-made man. Very modern.'

'It is terrible. He must be responsible. He adopted their son, and sent him here.'

'She made her own decision. Shima has contempt for death. She did what is natural for her.'

There was a deep aghast silence. It froze Anna: wealth, crime, business and politics come together in this new alliance, a new set of horsemen. She said, bleak at the prospect for all ordinary people, 'We seem to be moving into bad times, don't we?'

'Ah, you are so sure of right and wrong. People are the same everywhere. Money men are international, manipulation is everywhere, intrigue, self-serving, everywhere.' He looked up, his face expressing a kind of resignation, again sighed. He was small and tired, yet his odd-shaped features seemed to hold a sort of owl-faced wisdom. 'Hideo is modern young man. He is slave also to his past. Our people always so. The English also. You know, we once were forbidden physically to leave Japan on pain of death. Now it is mentally forbidden. Most Japanese cannot do it. They have to go back, or stay as half-people.' Was he talking of himself?

Had Shima been afraid Hideo wouldn't be Japanese enough, and what could she have discovered that reduced her to such despair?

'Shima was geisha, but a bit artist, a bit strange. The creative mind is peculiar. We Japanese don't like anything peculiar. We believe everyone should be the same.'

Anna was lost and stared out at the rain, made suddenly aware how the force of it had increased and that it was falling in straight rods like drawn glass, making a sound-curtain between them and the outside world; and close to, those individual drops of rain fused with others were rolling continuously down the windows.

'To try to hold onto something when it is breaking up, to try

195

to repair it is very English. English hold on. Japanese let go. We say, *shikata ganai*: it can't be helped.' He got to his feet.

But before she let him go she had to ask: would Kuneo see his son as still too independent, a rebel, and find some way to punish him?

'We have a saying: the huntsman does not shoot down the wounded bird.'

His umbrella had made a wet patch on the carpet. He clicked his tongue, and Anna's mind travelled back to the very first day and the snow, and saw the scene all over again, the spoon falling from the cup, the young man rigid on his chair. She shook her head.

Going gingerly down the steps, Mr Misumi started to put up the umbrella as he descended, and a gust of wind catching it he threatened to take off, but got control at the last minute, and she called down she hoped they'd meet again, but their words crossed. Had he said you've been a mother to him, or you've been a lover to him, she hadn't quite caught what it was, for turning he'd bowed to Anna, so that her last view of him was the black top angled towards her.

Anna thought of her now as the woman Miyako. Who had gone into the empty white space along with the unsaid and unseen which surrounded the strong black lines of this Japanese picture. How cruel it had been: she'd ceased being a mistress, she was no longer geisha, and she was not allowed to be a mother. All that Miyako had known of Anna was her voice with its bossy, western tone. Anna had known more; why had she never thought to send a message to this mother without her son? But she hadn't known, she whimpered to herself, she really hadn't known. Miyako had been a voice, a shadow too; had briefly taken on a solid presence in Anna's neurotic fancies, but now Anna was tormented by unanswerable questions: whether Otaki had given her Anna's address, whether he had tried to make her believe that Hideo had been 'kidnapped'. His function remained a mystery. And where had Hideo been? He'd been sent to a distant country to have a holiday and keep quiet while his father dealt with the serious threats to his stability and way of life, by any means possible.

The children when told about Louise looked askance and a little sly. Would Anna, you know, ever marry again, ever?

'I don't know. No one's asked.'

Shuffling his feet, Nick felt their father wouldn't like it somehow.

It had been some time since they'd mentioned Gregory. She never talked about him, so they didn't either. They were both looking solemnly at her, asking questions for which she had no answers.

'It's nice, isn't it, with Hideo here,' she said.

'It was better in the Lakes;' and they both fell silent as if confronted by a wall of rock.

The skies after all that rain were empty in a way they couldn't account for. There was something missing, and it took some time before they realized that it was the swallows which had gone, unnoticed. Some reparation was needed. They walked off to the cemetery where the children made a hole through the granite chips to the earth beneath, and planted there a strong white azalea.

*

Someone had told Hideo. As they entered the house you could detect it. He was coiled back tight inside himself, seated on the floor as if to put his body into the smallest possible space, hunched over, head sunk between his shoulders. Some field of force surrounded him so that she couldn't rely even on that western way of saying she was sorry, or touch him. Some time later when she came back still he'd not moved, but after she'd put tea before him she stayed sipping hers by the window, willing him to talk, seeing the way the clouds drove before the wind. But he wouldn't drink, only moved his shoulders irritably as he felt her eyes on him.

After a while she stirred. She would have to speak. 'Mr Misumi has told me about your mother.'

The clouds bunched and piled into each other. It would rain again soon. 'I am sorry.' She thought with envy of the swallows swooping before the clouds towards the warm air of Africa.

'*Watak'shi no.*' He said it under his breath. '*Kashitsu desu . . .*'

She waited.

'It was my fault.' All the colour had drained from his face, leaving it pasty.

'It can't be your fault. She was driven to it by the things your father was doing. She wanted to hide that.'

He looked up. His eyes were red. 'You use sharp words.'

'Sharp?' Her nerves were on edge.

'Your tone is harsh.'

'You can't defend your father, not after what you know.'

'He is my family now – '

'I can't believe it!'

' . . . I cannot hold my head up if I don't do – '

'Your mother's dead. And you still mean to go back?' She thought: he's learnt nothing then.

Sick at heart they sat together. Then Anna softly insisted he could do something, he must not accept. But he didn't make any reply.

Later still it had grown dark and there was nothing more to see and she drew curtains on the coming night, saw to the house and the children.

'No, he doesn't want to eat.' The children nodded solemnly. They knew what death meant and they crept nearer to Anna, so that she tried to jolly them a little; it was not their loss. But memories fatigued them so that they went early to bed and Anna sat alone as she had before, thinking. Okasan, the mother, had been a voice, an influence tugging gently (she saw now) but insistently on a sleeve. The woman Miyako, like many women impersonating the mother, the mistress, had also carried the idea of the perfect Japanese way of refinement too far. It had been impossible for her to sustain these changing roles: in the end it had been fatal.

Her feet had taken her without her conscious acceptance out again into the hall where she listened, straining her ears for any sound, and caught a reflection in the hall mirror; still there then – for she had felt these last few hours curiously disembodied, as if floating somewhere above her body, her fate floated with it.

'Yes, I understood when you said you were going back for her. But for him . . . And what of us, you and me?' She was stifled.

Hideo was lying on his back on the bed. He hadn't drawn the curtains, and outside one could hear the wind whipping round the corners of the house. The square panes were holes out into the night, but she dared not cover them. For some reason Hideo had taken out his father's knife and was twirling it in his fingers.

'It was body matter.'

She had a physical pain making her bend abruptly over her

199

knees: it was as if with one swipe he'd sliced out her heart. Tears prickled but she couldn't cry, rather she was chilled and trembling with the pain staying keenly near the breast-bone, and the beating of her heart thudding into her head. Slowly she straightened up, recognizing the grip of fear. No one who knows about rejection, about being alone, wants to go again into that black pit. Would a Japanese woman shout and shriek, or be contained and brave? Anna knew a small defeated smile had occupied her face. In the Lakes everything bad had been worth it for those days of closeness, for she knew now how she'd actually acquiesced and accepted at heart a premature ageing, and singleness, and he'd liberated her from that. That comfort remained. But it did not feel much.

Dazed, she went on looking at him. He was staring into some distance which did not belong to the room. Okasan had won then; in death if not in life she'd charmed him back.

Anna's trembling had to stop. She felt dirty.

'I suppose I should thank you for being so kind to me in the Lakes.'

'Oh not at all.' His tone had a cold politeness.

And she burst out violently: how could he talk like that – surely he hadn't forgotten – they had expressed love for each other – they had found joy, such pleasure together?

'We play. We were playing.'

He would not face her.

Anna turned her head away as if to look out of the window to steady herself, for all her experience of life had concentrated down to this small patch beneath her knees where she found herself kneeling back onto her heels. But the panes led out to nothing. Was this the way the East confronted the West, with the figure motionless before her on the bed? She put out her hand but he shook her off irritably and swung over until he sat above her on the edge of the bed. 'Nice place, *ne*? Nice holiday. We play games. Have fun, *ne*? Then forget.' And he retreated into his icy composure once more.

'I don't believe it,' she said quietly, 'not of you.'

Affairs, he said, just affairs.

Anna thought of his *Playboy*, his late nights in the town.

'Man and woman business, Mrs Dean.'

'Yes,' she said softer now, 'but this man and this woman.' The high windows rattled their window-panes. How dark it was.

'I am very sorry, Hideo-San. *Sumimasen.*' Instinct told her not to look at him, and to go away. She returned only with fresh tea which she put in front of him, lit a candle, and left him to himself.

He was getting his things together, and when she entered, worried he'd not eaten breakfast, nodded coolly and carried on. So, some recovery had taken place during the night; he moved quietly and with method, laying things out in a systematic way. Out of the corner of her eye she saw his English books. Anna wasn't interested any longer in sadness and sad endings: that was for the romantic past, when to be unhappy felt like living deeply. Now to live in some sort of content required far more effort, and far more courage. She kept her voice steady. 'You still don't have to go. At heart you know you were doing what your mother, not your father ordered.'

He turned swiftly, and his voice was terse. 'I endured staying on here but for what, you tell me that? You know we feel horror of going among unknown people – Oh,' he shook his head, 'it is useless.'

'You could disappear. Not go back. You were free in the Lakes, we were both free there, and we disappeared, we got away. Do it again.'

But his eyes seemed to show terror, as if she'd suggested a

201

form of annihilation. 'When I came here I felt that I had disappeared. It was terrible, Anna, when I first came here.'

Terrible? What had he hidden, that young man sitting on the edge of his chair, letting the spoon drop? She looked over at him, perplexed, pushing away the ignoble thought that he was exaggerating, and she thought how they'd fallen in love as individuals, and that then Hideo had actually been freed of Japan, just as she'd been freed from her guilty link with her husband's death. And yet they'd still brought with them their respective histories, tagging them along – like Hideo's luggage, now added to, she saw, by his clobber from the Lakes.

He sighed heavily. 'Japan will seem very crowded, Anna.'

Like an open prison.

'Were you very unhappy?'

He stopped what he was doing and looked hard at her, as if not trusting the question, then smiled. 'I was not unhappy after a bit.'

It was impossible to keep the children away. There had been tears, but now they stood around getting in the way and fingering things, Hideo being if anything more cheerful, but they frustrated Anna when she wanted to hold on to every minute.

The binoculars were on the desk and of course Nick had picked them up, and Hideo just said seeing this that Nick could have them, and that he could use them the next time they went to the Lakes.

Fay had turned a bright red, her lips pressed tightly, and Anna found that she'd looked away to the window – she often asked herself why she did this. To avoid confrontation, no doubt. Like the Japanese. She was furious with Hideo for his lack of sensitivity. 'They must share them.'

'Of course.'

But this wasn't good enough, and Nick's little smile of triumph stayed on his face as he lifted them, pointed over at Hideo. 'All the better to see you with.'

202

'Oh.' Hideo had heard the story, but he was not paying real attention. 'I know, Kitsune, in disguise.'

'No.' Fay said, prim but with a little pride in her voice at being able to correct, 'it's a wolf, not a fox, in disguise.'

Anna closed her eyes: it's his last day, she told herself, you've got to put up with it.

He was going to leave his English books behind. 'And these?' pointing towards several *Playboy* magazines. 'Off you go, you two.' But he grinned, taking one up. 'Oh, I think I take this for friend.' Yet his smile went and his face set into a mask.

'It's strange. I often think of foxes, now. Appearances are deceptive.'

And he frowned. He didn't understand.

'Things are often not as they seem. In love, and other matters.'

He had gone pale, she could not tell why. 'Anna, I give you the picture.'

Seeing again the woman cradling the man in her lap, with a new understanding Anna thought: once one has had a physical relationship then one is forever changed. Perhaps this was the message of the foxes.

'Don't you want it?'

'You keep it.'

'I don't think I will be able to hang it on the wall.' The men were just drunken sots, but the women were enjoying their mischief. Anna wished to God she could be amused by it. She slid the picture back into its tube; its power to disturb was too strong. And leaning against the window, gazing down into the garden, wondered where the fox could be. 'I wonder where it went?'

'Fox? How can you ask?' He had a very strange and guarded look on his face which she received, puzzled at what precisely lay behind it, and her skin prickled as the hairs rose on her arms. Over by the end of the garden where the dry, dead leaves lay in russet piles, was the place where they'd first seen the fox – didn't he remember? – it had been audacious, alert, scenting the air before slinking away. The foxes in those bad times had cunning enough to desert the country and move into the town. They are survivors and adaptable. The fox they'd seen then had appeared damaged standing out in the wintry cold because the white tip of its tail was lost against the snow. In her imagination now it was turning scarcely visible except for this white tip, as if with second thoughts, and was padding confidently forwards, until it disappeared into the house.

Hideo was frowning as if he wanted to say something but was held back, not by lack of words any longer but by the realization that here was something whose reality they knew to exist, but for which there were no concepts which did not offend the sense of what was true for him, or provable for her.

How odd it was. She'd asked that question in a jangle of nerves, carelessly, only to be thrust down into a deeper layer of meaning: it had the contrary effect of bringing them close once more. But there were no words, none, to ensnare such an elusive thing. It escaped.

So often in the past her mind had been fully occupied with domestic matters. Neither of them wanted this now, but like a nosy-parker, a busybody, details came pushing through: during this crisis of his mother's suicide, his laundry hadn't been done. Not to worry, but although he said this he gave every appearance of having lost his bearings, his ordering had gone and he began to throw things out, and throw things away.

'And what are these?' The sachets of white powder.

'Otaki gave me. I have allergy.'

'To animals? To cats?' To find this out the day before he leaves!

Anna left for the shops; she couldn't bear it, and the children were right, the house was a prison. The long way round took her past the house where Fay had gone for the afternoon, and past the college. Here she hesitated at the gate, and began almost automatically to go down the drive. The strange building was still lit by watery sun, but the cedar appeared blacker in the autumn light, and beyond it, at the far end, a gardener – an old man – was raking leaves which the wind, though slight, disarrayed from the heaps as he turned his back. He had taken no obvious notice of Anna's steps on the gravel, but as she studied the closed double doors, the windows lacklustre from atmospheric dirt, she heard him call out, 'All shut up. All gone.'

All gone?

There were changes too in the town where, struggling with a sense of the fickleness of things, Anna found that the new health-food shop had been transformed as if overnight into one which sold make-up; even the door position had moved so that Anna was faced with a wall of glass where she'd reached out for a handle. And as she stood nonplussed with no one to ask, it struck her how people looked grey and so sad; they seemed to have lost direction, their gestures as hesitant as hers. In the winter she'd seen the same crowd as predatory. The difference had to be in her. And she was altered, much altered. She stared until she was jostled into the stream of dispirited shoppers, aware now of undercurrents she'd ignored or mistaken before, and disturbing elements in everyday English life. That odd sensation of how it would feel to be used as an outpost of an empire, which she'd first experienced in the Lakes, came back, and as if to beat all her bounds and rid herself of a future that had no shape or purpose she could believe in, she set off again for the park, making her way stolidly over the boggy ground.

Over this ground where the wet flat leaves slid greasily over each other she paced, drawn on by a furious desire. Not to know – for that was impossible now – but to realize the full significance of this trodden round in which they lived. You could sit quiet in your earth, but you could also, for freedom, for complete living, take your chance out in the open.

They'd kept much at home since coming back from the Lakes, the contrast to the wild places being too cruel to put up with, and now that the trees were being peeled of their cover, the shape of the park with its opened-up copses, its flattened pits of dying bracken, appeared shrunk, and the trees on the higher exposed ground, some standing isolated, had grown – you could see now – cringing from the sharp winds. Down in the valley of the town Anna hadn't known what it was, but this unnerving vision of familiar places differently lit, of the familiar throwing unfamiliar and sinister shadows, must be what the wild animal experiences under chase. At this moment she identified her response: it was the feeling of living in occupied territory.

At the high spot on the road with the light failing, the sanctuary was to her right. Some ragged leaves caught her eye, and took her back to Clare's description of the three monks striding together. Just inside the metal palings of the sanctuary the first trees began. One could look deep through the bare branches and between the damp black trunks for some way; a heavy cover of dead branches and keeling-over bracken hid the floor of the wood. Memories chilled her. The palings were high and curved inwards to discourage trespass, but just outside, the clear sandy area was scuffed with marks, and there were several burrowed openings and the disappearing signs of tracks between the bracken stalks. It was the sign of foxes.

A large crow further in dislodged a yellowing leaf which floated through the gaps between the darkening branches. The only movement. It was hard to think of anywhere more deserted – even of ghosts. Though as she turned her back she ceased to know with certainty, as if the wood was waiting for the human to leave. It was only a trick of the light.

She ran clumsily and slipping on the hillocky ground in the darkness at her feet.

A note was waiting: I have gone to walk.

There were only a few hours more. A car would come for him, and then he would be gone. The night had rolled in swiftly, and the children lying before the television briefly smiling over at her were as if at the end of a long room that was not hers. She smiled back and paced the house.

There was a wind blowing up, catching the gaps round the window-panes which was what happened when the winds were northerly, and this produced a melancholy low moan. Intentionally not drawing the curtains, some of the light from the room stretched as far as the yew tree in the front garden. Swaying only slightly, it was solid enough to throw deep shadows. Fear and the self-centredness of grief cut one off from others and one missed a lot, making the picture of the world slanted and incomplete. Yet Anna recalled so clearly that first day, the two men waiting in the snow. She gave a rueful laugh.

'What! You laugh?'

He'd come back so silently – how had he got in without her seeing? She saw at once that he had the cold closed look, his pupils points of black in a deliberately narrowed slit-eyed inspection of her. He'd been in the back garden. Shrugged. It did not matter why.

*

It was very late. In twenty-four hours Hideo would be with his father, and Anna was thinking how Hideo in his present state of mind could easily kill him. He had gone demented that night in the Lakes as no other human she'd ever seen. But it was not for her to know what he intended to do. His face was set. Questions circled round her mind, tormenting.

He began muttering, '*Iye chigaimasu*. It is wrong.'

A mistake.

'To be sent round the world, and for nothing.' All a waste of time.

'You have learnt English,' subduing the pang that came.

'That is one good thing.'

Anna made a great effort, which felt at first as if she was trying to hold on to some substance in her arms while it was floating away, but then she became surer and tightened her grasp. 'No,' she insisted, 'oh no. I am beginning to understand you. The world can never be the same for me again. That for me does not mean waste. Your mother had you. You can carry on life for her.'

Did he follow her? He was saying nothing.

'We were both like children when you came.'

At the beginning, when it was just a matter of words, how simple it had been. There was no language but silence between them now.

After a while Anna got softly to her feet and turned out the lights. The trees were tossing to and fro restlessly. They could feel the eyes of Miyako watching from the garden.

*

So Otaki would accompany him back. Orders to that effect having been relayed earlier that morning; one call from Tokyo, one from London.

The Japanese way with presents had worked against the sorrow of the children, for Hideo had given them things of such magnificence they were almost stunned. Their behaviour was spontaneous, and right, and he showed himself touched, and they had made offerings of their own. How they were already growing up, growing away . . . they sprang from the house at a run, released through this gift of presents, believing in the lies of return.

The spare room upstairs that was still Hideo's room was scrupulously tidy except for the corner where the wastepaper basket stood. He'd thrown away clothes, books, his pencils. There was just a small packet on the table near the window. Anna could not account for the three modest pieces of unsewn cotton, printed in a grey geometric design.

'What is this?'

'That says name of store in Tokyo.'

'What are they?'

'Tea-cloths. For housewife. For you.'

A violent surge of anger – they could join the rest of the thrown-away stuff – was as suddenly followed by a hysterical desire to laugh. 'You brought these with you? From Japan.'

'They are leaving present.'

So it had all been planned. Anna, go down to your proper place.

He said quietly, 'Okasan bought them. She chose them.'

Okasan correctly had bought them for the woman who was

209

going to do the necessary tasks: to feed her son, and launder . . .

'Then I will keep them. In memory of her.'

They tried to talk of ordinary things, polite with each other, but whatever they mentioned had a devilish way of scraping against raw places.

Her eyes took in the correctness and style of the dark suit which set off the handsome oriental head and slim body. He held himself distant.

There were a few remaining leaves which the slanting sun lit from the side a brilliant gold. The tree planted at a focal point on their first planning of the garden had grown quickly. Anna had never watched its seasonal changes so keenly before, and now, waiting for the ring at the door, they both moved as if mesmerized to the window, gazing out as if for escape from the inner oppression, as if it would do some good. There was again a high wind this morning; the slender branches of the tree bent and twisted before it in a kind of manic dance, a tarantella of twigs, and with every gust more of the remaining leaves swirled off on the wind. They followed the movement away with their eyes, the glass no longer there. The journey out from the house had already begun.

Anna left Hideo to open the door, peering down from her room at the sleek black limousine drawn up outside (the new neighbours installing themselves were staring with interest), and she blessed her foresight in dressing for ceremony, for coming round the bend of the stairs there was an unpleasant moment as she took in that the man Sado and his fellow minder Honda were with Otaki. Anna saw no reason to hide her dislike, and by insisting on accompanying Hideo to the airport she was underlining how she was keeping up her protest to the very last minute.

The men stood rigidly to one side while the chauffeur packed the cases and then showed Anna first into the deep back seat, Hideo beside her, with Otaki. He was pale but

210

maintaining an almost silent dignity of bearing, and he avoided the looks from the two minders perched on their bucket seats facing him as the car pulled away from the house.

Anna had been near to tears; she had not expected to laugh or find a thing funny. Both Otaki and Sado wore dark suits, dark glasses. Honda had spoilt his effect she saw with some satisfaction, by wearing grey crocodile-skin shoes and a bright pink tie. His broad haunches were somewhat uneasily planted on the small bucket seat where he balanced, knees apart, like a sumo wrestler. Nothing could dampen his happy mood, not Otaki who sat tensely nor Sado who was very quiet. Anna thought she perceived much stress in the way Sado was gripping his kneecaps, which caused him once nearly to fall as they turned a corner sharply at some traffic-lights. She asked herself if he had any fear of return. Honda showed no concern at all; he was the only one talking: 'Have to go home. Be guddo boy.' He fixed his eyes on Anna. 'Had ngrish horiday. Good vacation. Much enjoyment time.'

The traffic being heavy, the car was moving forward slowly and in fits and starts, which had a worsening effect on Otaki's nerves for he reached hastily for cigarettes. Anna cried, 'Oh no!' and Honda with an obliging leer began to roll down the window so that the draft blew out the flame on the lighter in his hand.

'*Baka*!'

Honda grinned, and grunted out some Japanese while rolling the window back up.

Hideo had been silent, turned away from her. Now he spoke out: a curt order, it appeared to be. In amazement she saw Otaki put away his cigarette. 'Are you all right, Anna?'

'Yes. I am all right.'

'It does not take long.'

'I know that.'

Otaki had begun to take out documents from his briefcase, and was trying to instruct Hideo about something more complicated than mere arrival times. But Anna could see

211

that Hideo did not want to know. He moved his head impatiently and stared with a stony, fixed expression through the space between the shoulders of the two men.

The chauffeur was taking them through the back streets before joining the motorway. The lights were frequently against them, and Honda, grimacing through the car window at a crowd of shoppers waiting to cross, began a sort of chant 'Guddo bai, guddo bai . . .'

She had been feeling unhappiness pass over her repeatedly like waves of heat but she couldn't repress a snort of amusement at the look on the faces as Honda waved his pudgy fist. The first joints of two fingers were missing.

'*Kichigai onna*,' he said, '*kichigai gaijin*!'

What was that, she asked Hideo.

'Crazy 'ooman.' And Honda laughed aloud.

Crazy foreign woman.

Otaki had become insistent, leaning forward and speaking urgently in quick short sentences. But Hideo was, it seemed, oblivious; again he'd gone white and afterwards was alarmingly flushed. It was too much to put up with.

'Leave him alone! Isn't everything bad enough?'

Sado snarled something at her which was rude enough to stop Honda who was tapping his knee and grunting out some sort of song whose tune he was trying perhaps to find the end of.

'*Megitsune*!' The dislike in it made her recoil.

The word had made Hideo flinch and fix his gaze through the windows at the surburban houses, small businesses – Honda had been picking out the names of firms familiar to him and there were enough to keep him happy – small factories and garages, the inevitable flotsam of airports. The word sounded somehow familiar; some element in it Hideo refused to translate. Had it been so insulting?

'He called me a sly vixen then? It's an insult in English too,' and she began to laugh at the whole ridiculous irony, and again he turned away from her as if he found her laughter crude.

212

They were approaching the last quick stretch down the motorway when Hideo said suddenly, 'Anna-San.' It no longer mattered about the two opposite. Otaki still held the papers ready in his hand, and he kept his eyes on them; he was biting the side of a nail. Hideo had taken out his wallet – an uncomfortable moment while he searched among the banknotes – but it was a piece of paper he took out, handwritten in neat small blue script. 'It is poem. Miyako gave it to me. I will send you the words in English. They are from Heian time. She liked it!'

The car joined the motorway and quickly gathered speed. The others fell silent, each with their own thoughts; Anna so conscious of Hideo beside her, but Honda, again managing to do things his Japanese way – the unexpected – raised his voice once more. There was something horribly familiar about what he was trying to sing in spite of the distortion. He flashed a gold tooth at her. 'Good idea, *ne*?' he explained, nodding. He put his head back, oblivious or uncaring of his tight-lipped companions, and beating on his plump knees in time, out came the message on his unpleasant thick voice . . .

' . . . Orrud akwaint . . . be forgot . . . '

In the tunnel of the underpass leading beneath the runway, she leant her head back on the cushions in weakness and felt Hideo's look come swiftly to her, but as she moved her head he was again staring away. How could these last few moments . . . In what manner could they say goodbye? She'd seen the queues and the fuss of departure as diversionary, enabling them to be private in the middle of the crowds, but as the car drove smoothly into line she saw the back of the chauffeur adjust as he scanned the pavement and then pull forward with decision away from the customary stopping-place to where she grasped at the last minute there were one or two photographers waiting.

There was sudden action.

Sado now in charge, the men quickly got out; others rushing towards them. Anna last of all, gathering her wits with her handbag, was not quick enough. Sado's hand splayed flat

213

thrust her down into the deep seat. Outside Hideo had his back to her. The cases were being taken out with astonishing speed. The car door slammed on her and the chauffeur, somewhat irresolute, got back into the driving seat, half turning to Anna while making some signals to a traffic policeman: 'Where now?'

She'd slid to the side, her hand on the door—she must get out—when Hideo at last freed himself, for the moment only, from the others and looked for her. Otaki and Sado had by now placed themselves close either side of him.

The chauffeur started the engine. On Hideo's face clearly a resignation: it is inevitable. There is nothing we can do. Was he not going to say goodbye – the others seemed so anxious to hustle him away – or even bow in the Japanese manner? The two on either side looked like guards. She raised her hand. Through the back window she saw, or thought she saw him bow, but it could have been an unsteadiness for she saw his keepers' hands go sideways – for whatever reason – before the blackness of his head was lost among the others there.

'Where to, madam?' The car was gliding slowly away.

'I don't know.' The day stretched vacantly in front of her (she could feel Hideo moving numbly through passport control). 'How much is there on the clock?'

The things that perish are the more beautiful. She would not accept.

'I was booked for the day. It's all been paid for. You want to go shopping? Harrods? Visit the Tower of London?'

The car was approaching the motorway.

'You could go to Oxford and back if you like. You've seen him off, now you can see a bit of the old country. It's up to you.'

Something needed to be put into the day. It needed redeeming, making good.

Anna settled as comfortably as she could into the seat. She would open her eyes when the fields began.

'Let's do that then.'

214

PENELOPE FITZGERALD

Offshore

Winner of the Booker Prize

'This is an astonishing book. Hardly more than 50,000 words, it is written with a manic economy that makes it seem even shorter, and with a tamped-down force that continually explodes in a series of exactly controlled detonations. It is funny, its humour far more robust than it at first appears, but it has in addition a sense of battles lost, of happiness at any rate brushed by the fingers as it passes by, of understanding gained at the last second. *Offshore* is a marvellous achievement: strong, supple, humane, ripe, generous and graceful.'   Bernard Levin *Sunday Times*

Human Voices

'One of the pleasures of reading Penelope Fitzgerald is the unpredictability of her intelligence, which never loses its quality, but springs constant surprises, and if you make the mistake of reading her fast because she is so readable, you will miss some of the best jokes. I wish it were longer . . . for it is certainly a very funny novel about the BBC, and that in itself is an occasion for joy.'   Michael Ratcliffe *The Times*

Flamingo

Tim Parks

Loving Roger

'A tight, disturbing novel . . . mordantly illuminating on the way love contains the seeds of vindictiveness and hatred.'
Observer

'Extremely compelling . . . the human observation is witty, acute and sensitive . . . absolute authenticity.'
Sunday Telegraph

'With his chillingly elegant prose and frighteningly deadpan narrative, Tim Parks has written, not a whodunnit, but a brilliant whydunnit.'
Today

'A tale that is cruel, upsetting and compellingly credible.'
London Standard

Flamingo

Francesca Duranti

The House on Moon Lake

'An utterly original book and quite the most enjoyable I have
read in a long time'

Listener

'It is not until the terrifying climax that we realise that
Francesca Duranti's graceful and literary prize-winning
novel is really a horror story of the kind Henry James might
have thought of. I found it thoroughly scary'

Nina Bawden

'It is elegant and mysterious – a delicious book. It gave me
great pleasure, and I think it is the finest European novel I
have read this year'

Mary Flanagan

'*The House on Moon Lake* has won the Bagutta Prize, the
Martina Franca Prize and the City of Milan Prize. I wish
there were a prize we too could give it'

Independent

Flamingo